MY MOTHER
MURDERED THE MOON

NP Novellas:

MY MOTHER MURDERED THE MOON

Stephen Deas

NewCon Press
England

First published in the UK 2022 by
NewCon Press
41 Wheatsheaf Road,
Alconbury Weston,
Cambs, PE28 4LF

NPN015 (limited edition hardback)
NPN016 (paperback)

10 9 8 7 6 5 4 3 2 1

ISBN:

978-1-914953-12-5 (hardback)
978-1-914953-13-2 (paperback)

Cover layout and design by Ian Whates

Typesetting and editorial meddling by Ian Whates

Day One: 20:00 hours

'Wipe away the tears, wash away the blood, regrets are like a river, grief is like a flood…' Roxy sits at her desk, strapped into a swivel chair, head thrown back, singing like even the stars might sit up and take notice. The floor-to-ceiling screen behind her displays the view from the surface of Epimetheus, a hundred metres above her head: Saturn, occupying almost a quarter of the sky. Its rings beyond – Epimetheus orbits inside them – glitter in the light of the distant sun. They are dazzling and beautiful and immense, but she barely notices. She's been here a long time and the view never changes.

'But my love is like an ocean, unstoppable emotion, this feeling that I'm free, who I want to be…!'

At the second desk, positioned at a right angle to her own, Karl's hands are outstretched, his head tilted back, throwing himself into the song with the same unfettered passion, looking her in the eye as he does. He's somewhere in his thirties, Roxy's sort of age. Attractive in a doesn't-know-it kind of way with some pleasing bulges where muscular arms push against his skin-tight jumpsuit. They all work out because there's nothing much else to do out here. Roxy likes him, too, but neither of these things explains the singing. She can't remember how it started but it's peculiar to her and Karl. Major Nakita takes her duties as station commander too seriously for raucous singalongs. Also, Major Nakita can't carry a tune for shit.

It takes light an hour to reach Earth from where they are. Naki and Karl the only other human beings with whom Roxy can have a proper conversation. It also means, by unspoken agreement, that whatever happens on Epimetheus stays on Epimetheus. This includes bad singing.

On the wall behind Karl's head another screen shows a newsfeed from Earth. Around the entrance to the International Criminal Court in The Hague, protestors hold placards too distant to be read and chant slogans too indistinct to be heard. At the top of the steps, above the doors, hangs a huge screen. On it is projected a picture of the Moon. A reporter stands in front of all this, talking earnestly. His words are muted and lost under the singing. Roxy and Karl follow the song as the chorus repeats twice more, each with greater energy and vigour than the last. As the final chord crashes and fades, they fling their arms and faces to the heavens in unison, hold the last note until it dies, sneak a glance at one another, and then fall about laughing. They'll not win prizes at any karaoke night back on Earth, either of them, but that hardly matters out here.

The voice of the reporter pierces the new quiet, tinny but clear. *The Sea of Tranquillity mission started life in twenty forty-two as an offshoot of the International Lunar Staging Post mission, and as the starting point of the International Lunar Survey.'* The picture changes to a grainy shot of the Moon's surface and a single dirt-smeared dome, tiny against the vastness of the sea of dust that surrounds it.

'I hated that song even before I came out here,' Karl says, still chuckling, his face flushed with energy and joy.

'It hadn't been written when I left but I think I must have heard it before you started singing it at me. It's six years old now. Probably no one even remembers it, back on Earth.'

One of the first astronauts to work there, Marc Fremr, describes it in his biography as "little more than a mid-West garage with a handful of trucks and a couple of mechanics that just happened to be on the Moon".'

'Certainly not by the time either of us gets back.' Karl holds up both hands, each with his fingers crossed. By the time he and Roxy get back, she will have been gone ten years. Ten years evenly split between the cold-sleep transit out to Saturn, her duties as a Guardian of the Inner System, and then the cold-sleep transit back.

'Within the space of a decade, the world saw the explosive development of orbit-to-ground power transfer technology and the consequent development of the orbital reactors and solar capture arrays.'

Roxy starts chewing on a pencil she never uses for anything else, idly twisting her chair from side to side. 'So. This glitch of yours. Still there?'

'Irritatingly, yes.'

'And you're not seeing anything else out of whack?'

'Nope. It's weird.'

They both frown in shared concentration. For the last two days, Janus – by mutual consent, the crew's name for the Epimetheus Sentinel Station artificial intelligence – has reported a fault in its communications with two of the thirty-seven electromagnetic accelerators orbiting Saturn. The fault is constant but isolated to these two accelerators. Roxy has already managed to use the station's Artemis drone to connect to them, so the fault isn't with the accelerators themselves.

7

The demand for raw materials to be delivered into Earth orbit, the cost of launching them from the Earth's gravity well, and the availability of many of the same resources at a fraction of the cost from the lunar surface all led to the growth of what we now call the Sea of Tranquillity colony.' The picture of the Moon changes. The same sea of dust, but the one dome has become two dozen. A compact, thriving town in the vacuum of space. The image quality is excellent.

'Everything else looks entirely normal.' Karl offers an exaggerated shrug. 'The only thing I'm seeing that I haven't seen every single other day we've been out here is the Cronos.'

'…Twelve years ago, this was the largest gathering of human beings ever to exist outside the atmosphere of Earth, larger than the current Martian Colony programme…'

'Ah.' Roxy shakes her head. 'Still in the big man's shadow?' The big man being Saturn himself.

'She's in the final stages of orbital insertion on the inner edges of the rings. Not far from Janus, actually.' Janus also being the name of the big brother companion moon that shares Epimetheus's orbit and, by a weird quirk of gravitational mechanics, swaps places with it every four years. Giving the Epimetheus intelligence the same name was probably a mistake, but it's a confusion the crew have learned to live with.

'She'll be out of shadow on your shift,' says Roxy. 'I bet Naki insists on coming out to be the first to talk to them.'

Karl makes a face. 'Station commander's privilege. Maybe she can find out when they'll be finishing whatever they're doing out here. Maybe they could give us a ride home? Get us back early?' Karl makes no attempt to hide his enthusiasm. Epimetheus is a long posting in the loneliest place in the solar system.

'…The longest-serving members of its community had been on the lunar surface for more than thirty years…'

8

'Six more months. Then the *Voyager* will be here with the relief crew.' Roxy nods, absently. She looks distant, as if seeing an old familiar ghost lurking behind him, on the screen. Despite the isolation of this place, she doesn't share Karl's desire to return to Earth.

'*...It had a church and a mosque. It had a graveyard. It had a hospital. It had a school. Men and women of all nationalities lived their lives there, died there, were born there, many with neither the expectation nor desire to ever return to the world we call home...*'

'You okay?'

'*For them, for those pioneering men and women, the Moon was home.*'

Roxy shakes the feeling away. 'Sure. Hey, when we get back, first beer is on me, right?'

Karl sniggers. 'I know it's been a while, but Rox... Beer is for drinking, not for wearing.' He cringes, as if expecting Roxy to throw something, but she barely seems to have heard. The picture on the screen behind him is now a shot taken in low orbit over the Moon, looking down on the colony from above, a compact geometric arrangement of domes in tight concentric circles and a handful of outliers. A few kilometres from the main colony sit a trio of long narrow rectangular structures.

'Thanks, Karl. I mean I'll... Oh, you know what I mean!'

'Sure.' Now it's Karl's turn for hesitation, as if maybe he already has other plans. Roxy, who learned young to spot a half-truth, picks it up but lets it go.

She turns the news screen off.

'You get any chatter from Charlemagne about them?' Karl asks. 'The Cronos. They're early.'

'Two weeks.' Roxy gives a wry smile. 'Not much out of the three years to get out here. Probably some trivial error in the mass calculations. Charlemagne thinks they had problems getting everyone out of cold sleep.'

Karl shudders. 'They *lost* someone?'

'It didn't sound like it was that serious.'

'Well, what *did* they say?'

'Hardly anything. But she's supposed to be out here for more than a year last I heard, so no rush, right?'

'Sure, but when they come out of shadow, they'd better offer a bit more than here-we-are-this-is-our-proposed-orbital-insertion-trajectory-bye.' Karl makes a sour face. 'I mean, we've been out here long enough. I love you and Naki both but... Well, you know. Someone else to talk to now and then, that would be nice. A quick game of charades or something, maybe?' He frowns. 'If they're awake, they could already talk to us through the orbital relays, couldn't they?'

'Charlemagne probably hasn't given them access.' Roxy vents her frustration by spinning a full three-sixty on her swivel chair.

'You tried hailing them?'

'Sure.'

Karl shrugs. 'Maybe it's another fault, like the one on those two accelerators.'

'You know that's an entirely separate system.'

'Something wrong with the orbital relays.'

'Nope.'

'You sure?'

Roxy gives a condescending smile. 'You angling to take Artemis for another joyride? You know Naki won't let you. You *do* remember the last time, right?'

Janus and Epimetheus race around Saturn once every sixteen and a half hours in almost the exact same orbit. Almost, but not quite, which means that every four years, whichever one is faster catches whichever one is slower. Instead of colliding, they slingshot each other, switching places, the slower moon becoming the faster and vice versa. Four years later, they catch up with one another and do it again. Over and over, changing places, regular as a clock. At their closest approach, their separation is about fifteen thousand kilometres, well within the range of Epimetheus's Artemis drone. The last time it happened, two years ago, Charlemagne asked them to send Artemis to survey Janus, looking for a potential site for a second sentinel station. This had led to Karl's brief and half-baked plan to use the drone to carry him out there, suited up, to be the first man to stand on Saturn's innermost moon. He'd been suited up before Naki discovered what he was up to. She still hasn't quite forgiven him.

'Oh, do get lost!'

Roxy raises an eyebrow. 'Munchausen Syndrome again, is it? With an AI-driven railgun capable of throwing hundred-ton rocks at a large fraction of the speed of light? Not a great look, you know.'

'What are they going to do? Fire me?' Karl looks around the room behind him. 'Hey. Janus! Give me the last diagnostic report on the accelerators. Loudly, so my sceptical colleague here can hear.'

A disembodied voice speaks in a calm, neutral tone. 'Accelerators four and eight are not responding, Commander. All other accelerators report normal completion of tests.'

'I'll Munchausen *you*!' Karl glares but his eyes are smiling. Roxy laughs.

'Janus, repeat your last self-test summary for the orbital relays, please. Loudly, so my neurotic colleague here can hear?'

The same disembodied voice speaks again. 'All relays are operating within normal expected tolerances, Commander Micah.'

'Links via relays to the accelerators?'

'All functioning correctly.'

Roxy gives Karl a pointed look. 'No joyrides for you. Maybe we've got another hole in one of the antennas?' That happens, especially this close to the outer edges of the rings. Janus and Epimetheus are in a clear zone, carved out from the debris that forms Saturn's ring system by their own gravity, which is why they were chosen; but the large-scale stability of Saturn's rings doesn't preclude the occasional aberration, and small meteor strikes are common nuisance.

She raises an eyebrow. 'My shift's about done. Guess *you're* the one who's going to have to go outside, then.' Neither Roxy nor Major Nakita are particularly keen on walks around the surface of Epimetheus. Even the mildest agoraphobia struggles with the emptiness up there, with the sheer size of Saturn dominating a full quarter of the sky.

'I am, aren't I.' Karl, on the other hand, has no such fears. It's almost as though he likes it out there.

'Any excuse, eh?'

'Any excuse.'

'Good luck, then. Stay safe.'

'I will. See you later for shots?'

Roxy smiles at that. 'Sure will.'

Day Two: 0700 hours

Roxy lies in bed in her cabin. Soft music is playing, telling her it's time to get up, suit up, eat the first meal of another artificially manufactured day and take her shift. Each shift is sixteen hours, with eight hours allocated in between as a sleep period. This arrangement ensures that there are always two crew members awake and active. While on-shift, Roxy is required to be on duty in the command centre for ten hours, the other six being allocated for recreation, exercise, and personal time. In practice, aside from the two mandated hours each day in the exercise room fighting the constant battle against muscular atrophy in this close-to-zero gravity environment, all three of them usually end up in the command hub. There simply isn't anything else to do.

She sits up. As soon as she does, the disembodied voice of Janus speaks. 'Commander Micah, I have received a message from General Micah. Would you like me to play it now or archive for later?'

Roxy hesitates. General Micah is both her commanding officer and her mother, and Roxy never knows in what capacity she will appear, or whether the general even sees a distinction between the two. Right now, because of what's happening on Earth, her mother is passing her time on the European Space Agency orbital command hub, official designation ESS-03, unofficial designation: Charlemagne Station.

'Play it,' she says, because if life has taught Roxy anything, it's that an unpleasantness faced is an unpleasantness you can put behind you.

The screen lights up. Roxy doesn't look, not that there's much to see. A woman twice her age yet with a passing resemblance, severe and in the full uniform of a general.

'Commander Micah, please contact the Cronos immediately on receiving this. The Cronos has cleared Epimetheus to piggy-back onto their QIF array and establish a real-time link to the Charlemagne. You are instructed to notify command when the link has been completed. Please be reminded that the Cronos is not an ESA asset and that all communications routed this way are to be considered insecure. Communications requiring disclosure of classified information are to be maintained via existing protocols. Micah out.'

'The message is flagged as requiring an immediate response,' says Janus. 'Would you like me to open a channel to the Cronos?'

Roxy stares out into the void. 'No. And if my mother calls again, please tell her I'm in my sleep cycle, with instructions not to be disturbed. Let her leave another message.'

'Commander Micah, you are not in your sleep cycle. I cannot give information I know to be incorrect.'

'Then tell her I don't want to talk to her.'

'General Micah is our superior officer. We must comply with her orders.'

'When the Cronos makes contact, establish the link.' Roxy hasn't been entirely honest with Karl. It's true that she hasn't had contact with the Cronos via the orbital relays, but this is because she hasn't tried. She stares out at the image of Saturn and his rings, projected onto the wall of her cabin in lieu of a window, the same image that gets projected everywhere in this forsaken place. 'Janus, search through the moderated feeds from Earth. Everything from the last twenty-four hours. Keywords Sea of Tranquillity massacre, trial, war-crimes and verdict.'

It was always coming, this day. Not that knowing in advance has made it any easier.

Janus processes this, then: 'I have seventeen results. They have a high degree of correlation. Broadly, the commentaries fall into two categories: predictive and reflective. How would you like me to sequence them?'

'Merge the predictive into a summary and play me that.'

The image of Saturn and its rings vanishes from the wall, replaced by a reporter standing in front of a tall expanse of tinted glass, of brilliant white concrete and of marble columns. The same building as depicted on the screen behind Karl, back when he and Roxy were singing.

'...here in front of the International Criminal Court in The Hague, where in just a few days we expect the presiding judge to present a verdict on what has been described as the trial of the century: the prosecution of civilian and military officials for the Sea of Tranquillity Massacre...'

The scene cuts to a talking head in a studio. '...in which over three hundred lunar colonists lost their lives...'

'They didn't "lose their lives,"' says Roxy. 'They were murdered.'

'... the court has heard testimony from all levels of personnel involved in the crisis and in the events and decisions leading up to and including the fateful order to turn the Near-Earth Asteroid

Deflection Railgun Array, NEADRA, against the self-declared independent lunar colony, testimony ranging from state representatives of the United Nations Security Council nations responsible for the decision to disable the lunar mass drivers, down to the NEADRA duty staff officers immediately responsible for receiving and executing the order to fire on the lunar habitat. Much of this testimony has been received behind closed doors, with critics of the massacre vocal in protesting…'

The video switches to a third news reporter, outside again, but now the backdrop is the unmistakeable outline of the European Space Agency headquarters and primary launch and recovery site: Kourou in French Guiana, which over its century of history has grown into a small city of a hundred thousand people, half of them locals. '…in order to protect the identities of both themselves and their families against threats of retribution from relatives of the victims, branded by some as terrorists following the car-bomb assassination two years ago of Alessandro Serpicha, president of the European Space Agency at the time of the massacre…'

Another cut, back to the reporter standing outside The Hague. 'In the final week, carried out in public and on camera, the court received testimony from relatives of victims of the atrocity. The court also publicly heard the infamous and much debated recording alleged to have been made by the first astronauts to visit the site in the aftermath of the attack. While many questions remain over the authenticity of the so-called Hellscape tape…'

The scene changes to a static picture of the Moon. A new voice speaks. And here it is. *That* tape. *That* recording, an alleged interview with an ESA astronaut, carried out in secret, months after the massacre. The voice is calm and steady, but the interview has been spliced over a soundtrack of pops and crackles and the occasional muffled radio-call.

'We landed two days after the attack. We were just regular astronauts, most of us.' Hisses and a crackle and then an indistinct voice on a static-filled radio *I got body parts.* 'There were a couple of us who'd been in the services before they signed on. They'd seen action in Central America at some point, I think.' *Confirmed. Definite body parts.* 'They didn't talk about it but... Well, anyway, it didn't make any difference. Nothing could have prepared us for what we found.' *A leg and a torso, I think.*

'The habitat was shattered. Two of the modules took direct hits. There wasn't much left of those. I suppose the people caught inside those were the lucky ones. For them, it was instant.' More crackles and pops of static. *At least three casualties here. Three torsos with partial limb attachment. I don't know what the fuck happened but none of them have got heads.* 'The others... I don't know exactly how to describe it. It must have been the shock of the impact. They were ripped apart. Just... torn to pieces. And the people inside them... I supposed explosive decompression got them. Most were literally ripped to shreds.'

More static. *Body parts here as well. Two confirmed adults.* 'Someone tried to explain it, after we got back and told them what we'd seen. The shockwaves from the impact through the lunar surface just... turned them into jelly. And then the decompression came and ripped them apart.' *I got more here. I don't know what.* 'We found parts... scattered across the lunar surface. We tried to recover as many as we could. I remember one of us coming back with a severed head, with icicles of blood hanging off it.' *Oh Jesus fuck.* 'Terrorists? I don't know.' *It's a fucking kid. It's a fucking kid!* 'Maybe some of them, but...'

17

As the speaker pauses, the background cuts to silence, dropping the next words into a void that only serves to make them louder. 'They told us all the families had been evacuated on the Sullenberg, but it wasn't true. They were still there.'

'Stop.' Roxy holds her head in her hands. 'Just stop.'

The recording stops.

'Would you like me to create a synopsis of the reflective pieces, Commander?' asks Angel. 'They provide a detailed summary of the events leading up to the trial and…'

'No. I know what happened.'

Day Two: 0930 hours

Everyone is in the command hub when Roxy enters, which is to say that both Major Nakita and Karl are there, which is hardly a crowd. Still, shift patterns being as they are, it's relatively uncommon for all three crew of the Epimetheus Sentinel Station to be up at once. Naki looks fresh. Karl looks exhausted, streaks of stale dried sweat on his jumpsuit.

'You been outside?' Roxy asks.

Karl gives a wry smile and nods the wall-screen. Instead of the usual image of Saturn from the surface, the screen displays a frozen image of the International Criminal Court in The Hague.

'Jesus,' hisses Roxy. 'You're watching that too?'

Before Karl can reply, Naki takes a step closer. 'Everyone is watching. Everyone here and everyone on Earth, too. Have you heard the news?'

For a moment, Roxy's urge is to run. 'News?'

'About the verdict.'

'They've issued a verdict? Already?' Now she *really* wants to run. 'I thought that wasn't coming for at least another week!'

Naki is shaking her head. 'Not yet. But they've brought it forward.'

'Two days is what they're saying now,' says Karl; when Roxy looks at him, he's looking past her, at the screen, like he's somewhere else. 'They announced it just after you went off shift.'

'Two days?'

'That they won't find anyone guilty,' he says. 'They should but that they won't.'

Which is exactly what Roxy thinks, but she knows she can't say so.

Naki cocks her head and wags an angry finger. 'Why do you say that?'

'What? You think they will?'

'Commander Veers!'

Karl shakes his head. 'Sorry. I'm just exhausted.'

'You know Roxy's mother is General Micah?' Roxy winces because yes, of course Karl knows that. She told him, years ago. *Everyone* knows.

She steps between them, before this can get any worse. 'Then you both know she was the NEADRA duty officer that night,' she says. 'And you both know she was the one who executed the order to fire on the Moon.' Roxy closes her eyes, pushing through painful memories. 'I happen to agree with Karl that she should have refused the order. That's why she sent me out here. To get rid of me.'

There. As her grandmother used to say, better out than in. She checks their faces. Karl looks a little mournful, like he's sorry to have brought this up. Naki looks shocked.

'I thought you had to volunteer for this,' Naki says. 'Don't you?'

'Not if you have someone with enough clout to pull some strings and do the volunteering for you.' Roxy spits the words, filled with bitterness. 'I don't mind. In a way, she did me a favour. It's quiet out here. She can't reach me if I don't want to be reached.' Three years and she's never spoken about this to Naki, only to Karl. Naki, despite being the senior officer, is the newbie, only a year on-station. Maybe that's why.

'Lonely, though,' says Karl.

Roxy's turn to shrug. 'Naki's here because she's half German, half Japanese and has more sense of civic duty that the whole of North America put together. I'm here because my mother murdered the Moon. What about you, Karl. What are *you* running from?'

Karl smirks. 'I'm not running from anything! This is a plum post. Three years to get out here, four years on duty with nothing to do but watch porn and old movies, three years to get back. Sure, it sucks being stuck in the middle of nowhere, and I guess going back after a whole decade is going to be a bit weird, but the pay... I mean, that's ten years on top tier, and no way to spend any of it. I can practically retire when I get home.'

'Sure.'

'No, seriously. It's going to be fast cars and loose women all the way for Commander Karl when I get back.' Karl grins, but then takes a deep breath and looks away, as if he was considering letting something out and has thought better of it.

'Hey! Roxy!' Naki's holding her hand to her cheek, thumb and pinkie extended. 'Call for you. It's Canada. They want a word.'

Roxy cocks her head. 'Excuse me? Time lag!'

'You hurt their feelings enough they invented time travel.' Naki holds her other hand to her other cheek, same gesture. 'Oh, and I've got Mexico on line two.'

A moment of silence, and then Karl sniggers, and Naki is smirking, and Roxy has to give in and smile as well. Naki can be a bit distant, but there's a reason she was sent here and put in charge.

'Fine. Tell Canada and Mexico that I'm sorry.'

Naki makes a show of turning to each of her imaginary phones. 'You hear that? She takes it back. We all good?' She nods. 'Canada says you're good. Mexico's still thinking about it.' She flicks a glance to Karl. 'Want to tell Commander Micah what you told me?'

'The problem with those accelerators? You figured it out?' Roxy asks.

'Blown relays. Both of them.' Karl lets out a long sigh and rolls his eyes and then grins. 'Can you believe that?'

'Blown relays? How'd *that* happen?'

'The antennas are all powered by the main grid, right? But they all have small battery packs too,' says Naki. 'The batteries are to allow on-site testing before connection to the main grid. Once each antenna is hooked up, the batteries are supposed to be physically disconnected.'

'Four and eight were still live,' explains Karl. 'Whoever ran the set-to-work tests forgot to disconnect them.'

'The batteries are long past their end-of-life dates. They're degrading. They were causing power spikes.'

Karl rolls his eyes. 'Trivial enough to fix, but I had to go and check every single one of the other antennas to make sure they didn't have the same problem. I can confirm the set-up batteries are *definitely* all disconnected now. Took forever but it's done. Links to all the accelerators are fine now.'

They're laughing, but the idea of something so simple suffering a malfunction, and that it needed Karl to go outside to fix it, strikes Roxy as wrong. Three years and they've had their share of faults, but nothing like this. The Epimetheus Sentinel Station is designed for nothing if not to keep its astronauts safe. The sheer expense of them, their distance from Earth, the difficulty of relief, the impossibility of evacuation, all these things dictate both a skeleton crew and a design to minimise the probability of any incident. And, as every astronaut knows, the probability of something going seriously wrong gets about a thousand times higher the moment you suit up and go outside. This close to Saturn's rings, outside is never safe.

'You want to go out and double-check?'

'No one's doubting you,' says Naki.

'No, sure, but...' Roxy turns to Naki. 'You're going for a full inspection, right? Top to bottom diagnostics. Report the whole thing? It's not like we've got anything better to do with our time.'

'Of course. It's standard procedure.'

'I'd like to see the results. An installation mistake like this... It shouldn't have been possible.'

Naki nods. 'You'll both see them.'

Karl is nodding too. 'Yeah. Someone in the design department screwed up for sure. Look, while we're on the subject, I think we ought to take those accelerators out of the network and run a calibration. I know the next scheduled full-system shake-down isn't due for another month but... I'd like to be sure. A blown relay means an electrical glitch which means who knows what the last few packets were to get sent. What do you think, Major?'

Naki takes a moment. Live firings require the consent of all crew members. Throwing a large rock across the solar system at a substantial fraction of the speed of light demands an authorisation code from Earth, the primary fail-safe, but Janus doesn't require such a code for a calibration and test cycle, and so the need for Karl and Roxy and Naki to agree is no token gesture.

'Agreed,' says Naki. 'I'll set it up. Commander Micah? Would you like to join me on the hub to do the honours?'

'Sure. Go ahead. Just don't have me hit anything that matters.'

Naki turns her attention away from Roxy and Karl for a moment. 'Janus? Major Nakita Subaru. Confirm identity.'

'Confirmed,' says Janus.

'Authorisation to take accelerators four and eight autonomous for the next fourteen hours for the purposes of conducting a calibration exercise. All boundaries remain at their default safety settings. Valid calibration targets are limited to Saturn's main planetary body.'

'Access confirmed.'

Roxy and Karl repeat the mantras. When all three have given their permission, Naki offers them each a little bow. 'Commander Veers, I know you like to be present whenever we fire an accelerator, but on this occasion, I think you'll have to miss out. You're overdue some rest which you very clearly need. I'll have Janus extend your sleep period to compensate. Commander Micah and I will cover.'

Karl returns a grateful nod. The command hub doors hiss softly as they open to let him leave. Naki cocks her head to Roxy.

'Commander? Shall we?'

'You want to throw some rocks about?'

'Indeed, I do.' Naki smiles. 'When we're done, take some private time. We've established communications with the Kronos. Charlemagne needs to talk to you on a personal matter.'

Roxy closes her eyes. She nods. However hard she tries, she can't put it off forever.

'It's been nice having you for company, Commander.'

'And you, Major. But you've still got me for another six months.'

'Not according to the Cronos.'

'*What?*'

Naki makes a helpless gesture. 'I'm just the messenger. Talk to Charlemagne.'

Roxy, who knows perfectly well that the first face she'll see will be her mother's, can only nod. She settles at one desk while Naki settles at the other. Together, they begin the power-up sequences for accelerators four and eight.

Day Two: 2030 hours

Roxy sits in her cabin. Shift done, calibration complete. Karl is in the command hub, disappointed they're not doing pretend shots together; but Roxy isn't in the right place for that, not tonight. She's put it off and put it off, but as she tells herself over and over, an unpleasantness faced is an unpleasantness she can start putting behind her.

She taps a button. The cabin wall goes back to showing Saturn and its rings instead of the reportage from The Hague. She sits in silence, waiting. She doesn't want this, but what can she do? The combination of mother and superior officer is overwhelming. Some shadows can't be escaped.

When the screen flickers and changes, General Micah presents herself, taut and inflexible. Roxy stares back, not sure what to expect. For the last three years, every conversation traded with her mother has been a stream of monologues, the reply to each arriving two hours later. The two of them haven't had a proper conversation since before she left Earth, six years ago. A reasonable argument could be made that they hadn't had a proper conversation back then, either.

'General.' Roxy salutes, sits stiff and straight. 'Commander Micah, reporting as ordered.'

The delay is enough to notice, not much more than a second but long enough to see the barb hit its mark, how it makes her mother flinch. The miracle of Quantum Temporal Interferometry – QIF – made possible by the work of the Indian genius Doctor Rakhi Chandrasekhar and her breakthrough ideas that have led to, among other things, Simulation Theory. The same Doctor Chandrasekhar isn't far away right now. According to the crew manifest, she's aboard the Cronos.

'Roxy...'

'Commander Micah. Ma'am.' With anyone else, she might have said more. Shown her amazement at being able to talk like this. But not here. With her mother, she stays rigid, still, silent and without expression. A soldier in front of a superior officer. Nothing more, nothing less.

'Fine.' Her mother's face tightens a little more. 'Have you spoken to the Cronos?'

'No, ma'am. My instructions were to contact Charlemagne as soon as the link was available. I intend to contact the Cronos after we're done and thank them for their assistance.'

'Your deployment is being terminated early. The Cronos will relieve you while she's on station. You'll transfer directly to Earth. They have the details for you.'

'With respect, ma'am, how, exactly? Unless her mission profile has changed, the Cronos is on station for a minimum of eighteen months. She'll still be here when *Voyager* arrives.'

'The Cronos is a collaboration between private finance and NASA. Other than delivering an ESA payload to Epimetheus, she has no affiliation to the agency and her mission is neither your concern nor mine. Nevertheless, thanks to the payload she's delivering to Epimetheus, you'll be home before the end of the year.'

For a long time, neither of them speaks.

'I thought Karl and I were coming back with the *Voyager*,' says Roxy, when she's finally able to break the silence. 'Another six months here. Then three more years in transit.'

'Commander Veers will return when the relief crew on the *Voyager* arrive, as planned. You'll be returning on your own. The Cronos is carrying a self-powered acceleration pod. Once deployed, it will guide itself to Epimetheus station. You will board it and pilot it to your first stage accelerator. You will be provided with a trajectory, which you will use to programme the Sentinel accelerators. The accelerators will fire you towards Earth. The NEADRA orbital accelerators will catch and decelerate you at this end. It's not going to be a tenth of the speed of light, more like a few ten thousandths, but it cuts the transfer down from three years to three months. You'll be in cryo-suspension for the duration. You won't feel a thing. I just want you home, Roxy.'

Roxy considers this. Her mother's last words ring false; and anyway, does she *want* to go home? Not really.

'And the *Voyager*?' The *Voyager* left Earth two and a half years ago, not long after Roxy arrived. On board are two astronauts and supplies for another ten years of operations on Epimetheus. Two astronauts who were supposed to trade places with her and Karl.

'Proceeding as planned.'

'I'll have to confirm that with my commanding officer, ma'am.'

'Major Nakita already has her orders, Commander.'

'And she's okay to run Epimetheus with only two crew for a whole six months?'

'It's dangerous out there,' her mother says.

'More so if we're short-handed, ma'am. It's also dangerous at home,' says Roxy. 'Especially for me.'

'What's that supposed to mean?'

'You know exactly what that means. Ma'am.'

General Micah's turn to pause. 'This whole business will blow over long before you get back.'

'No, it won't.'

'Yes, it will. The trial will prove that everything was done correctly. The chain of command was followed precisely. A legal order was given. Everyone followed their instructions to the best of their ability. What happened on the Moon will be explained away as malicious intervention by parties unknown. That's where the attention will go. Beyond that, people will start to forget. Not the lunars, of course, but with everything out in the open, the rest of the world will move on. And when it comes down to it, who *are* the lunars nowadays? A few hundred people barely scraping a living in orbit? No one will listen to the relatives of terrorists who held the Earth to ransom.'

'There were children.'

'No, Roxy, there weren't.'

'Please address me as Commander Micah, ma'am. And ma'am, almost everyone on Earth must have heard that recording by now.'

'The hoax they call the Hellscape tape?' General Micah spits her disdain. 'Roxy, it's a fake. All of it. ESA sent sixteen astronauts to deal with the aftermath. You know that perfectly well. You know their names, you know most of them personally, and almost every one of them has testified that the recording is a lie. When the verdict is given, that part of the trial will be made public, and that will be the end of it. There were no children. Only terrorists.'

'You know that's not true.'

'I know it *is* true.' General Micah checks her watch. 'I have to go but I'll talk to you again before you leave. Liaise with the Cronos about the schedule for your return.'

Roxy continues looking into the monitor long after it goes dark.

Day Three: 0745 hours

Roxy is eating breakfast in what she and Karl have taken to calling the social club, the one room on the station where the three of them sometimes hang out together that isn't the command hub. She's alone this morning. Karl is asleep and Naki is going through the results of yesterday's calibrations and running through the results of the diagnostic checks on the repaired antennas. Breakfast is the same slurry of carefully balanced proteins, vitamins and minerals Roxy has had for the past three years. Perversely, and to the horror of both Naki and Karl, Roxy rather likes it.

'Commander Micah.' Janus suddenly speaking makes her jump. 'I have Chief Scientist Doctor Rakhi Chandrasekar from the Cronos asking to speak with you. Shall I accept the connection in your private quarters?'

Less than a minute later, Roxy is sitting on her bed, wiping her mouth, face lit with astonishment. *The* Doctor Chandrasekhar? In all honesty she'd be happy to talk to almost anyone right now, anyone to take away last night's bitter taste of her mother.

The face on the monitor changes to that of a small middle-aged Indian woman who apparently suffers an almost pathological inability to sit still. 'Commander –'

'Roxy. Call me Roxy.'

'Roxy. Yes, yes, good, fine. I'm –'

'Doctor Chandrasekhar. Astrophysicist, quantum gravity theorist, former Deputy Chief Scientist at the Indian Space Agency, chief scientist for the Cronos mission.' She's making a fangirl fool of herself, she knows, but can't seem to help herself. 'I know who you are, Doctor.'

'Rakhi, please –'

'You lectured at European Space Agency Academy in 2065. That was my graduation year. I remember your talks on quantum time and space...' Roxy forces herself to breathe. 'I'm sorry. It's... I don't have many conversations with actual real people out here.'

Rakhi Chandrasekhar flashes a glittering nervous grin. 'I am delighted to find myself so well remembered to an astronaut of the European Space Agency military. Although I must tell you to forget most of what I said in those lectures. Science moves ever-onward.'

'Well... I don't think any of us really understood what you were teaching back then.' Roxy swivels in her chair. 'We were astronauts, not physicists. But stuck out here for the best part of three years with nothing to do... I know the first real experiments into quantum temporal interferometry were done by the Chinese, but it was *your* theory behind them. I just had a conversation with someone across a billion kilometres. It should have taken hours for her to ask me a question and for me to reply but it was almost as though we were in the same room.' Roxy grins. Finally, a chance to talk about something she enjoys, and with someone she respects. She hasn't missed Earth, if you add it all and balance it, but she *has* missed this. 'In time, every astronaut will remember you, Doctor.'

'The QIF array is the work of many people.' Doctor Chandrasekhar beams nonetheless. 'Commander... Roxy... Have your people briefed you about your proposed return to Earth?'

Roxy nods. 'I've had a summary.'

'The pod to carry you will depart the Cronos shortly. It will take most of two days to reach you. Its self-propulsion ability is limited, so the trajectory will be an orbital one, relying on Saturn's gravity to do the work. I'll run the calculations again once we're properly inserted and give you a more precise time.' She hesitates. 'I know it's not my business but, well... but what a view you have! I can't stop staring at it.'

Roxy turns, taking in the sight of Saturn and its rings projected on her wall. 'You get used to it after a while.'

Doctor Chandrasekhar purses her lips. 'I make it my policy to speak with only the utmost politeness to anyone who has at their disposal the capability to fling many tonnes of iron at a significant fraction of the speed of light in any direction they choose. Nevertheless, I don't believe that what you say can be possible.'

Roxy grins back. 'I would have said the same about your quantum interferometer.'

Chandrasekhar laughs, a little nervously. 'Commander... may we discuss the means by which you will return home?'

'If I've understood correctly, you want to fire me back to Earth using my own railgun.'

'*I* have no wish one way or the other in this regard. In fact, I am required to inform you that this matter is not endorsed in any way by either NASA or the FusionFire corporation, nor indeed any other entity, either private or state, supporting the Cronos mission.' She looks and sounds very serious. Roxy snorts.

'Okay. *ESA* wants to fire me back to Earth using my own railgun.'

'The calculations appear sound. You will be travelling at close to one tenth of one percent of the speed of light. The asteroid defence network around Earth will capture your capsule and establish you in a stable Earth orbit.' As she speaks, Chandrasekhar fidgets and drums her fingers. 'Commander... Roxy. Are you aware...?'

The truth hangs between them, unspoken until Roxy breaks the silence. 'Am I aware,' she says, 'that no one's done this before?'

Chandrasekhar's nervous ticks grow more pronounced. 'Commander... I consider it a duty as a scientist to review the information I'm obliged to supply. I cannot deny that simulation testing has been thorough. Tens of thousands of iterations. It is one of our mission objectives to assess the use of your facilities to deliver ice from Saturn's rings to the Mars terraforming projects. But... If this were *my* experiment, I would carry out my first demonstration using something more inert and less valuable than a human life. I suppose I am wondering... if there is a reason for this *haste*.'

Roxy silently agrees, although the reason is so trivial as to be banal: her mother wants her back. 'Thank you, Doctor Chandrasekhar, but I can't discuss that.'

'Rakhi, please.'

'Thank you... Rakhi. Your objection is noted. And appreciated.'

'Of course... If your return to Earth is a success, there is no denying it will transform our exploration of the outer worlds. The

Cronos is capable of almost indefinite self-sufficiency. Using the accelerators here and around Earth, we have the potential to establish a permanent presence in the outer system.'

Roxy nods. She's already been thinking on this. 'If transit times can be reduced to a few months, astronauts can work in the outer system on the same eighteen month shifts as they already work in orbit.'

'And every world will become accessible thanks to your pioneering voyage. Perhaps your future astronauts will remember *both* our names?'

Roxy feels her cheeks burn. 'I'm only the passenger.'

'So was Gagarin.' Chandrasekar smiles and then leans away from the screen and turns her head, as if looking at someone out of view. 'I'm sorry, I have to go. I'll be in touch again when our orbit is established. Cronos out.'

Day Three: 1430 hours

Alone in the command hub, Roxy taps on her monitors. The view from the wall-screen changes and splits into two. One half stays the same; in the other, Saturn is even larger than he looks from Epimetheus, though he's only present at the edge of the screen, his rings not much more than an arc of light in the distance through space. The view is from one of the Sentinel accelerators. Major Nakita is asleep, as is Karl, his shift extended in preparation for later, when Naki plans to go back outside. Ostensibly, this is for another manual inspection of the accelerator antennas following a reply from Charlemagne to their diagnostic information; but Naki took the communication from Charlemagne in her private quarters and hasn't shared its contents, which is rare. Three people trapped together in a tiny space for more than a year get to know one another well. Both Roxy and Karl understand there's something Naki isn't saying.

A third wall-screen lights up, an orbital map of Saturn, highlighting the thirty-seven accelerators that are the point and purpose of Epimetheus Sentinel Station and its mission to deflect anything from the outer system, up to and including the size of a comet, that might be on a trajectory to threaten Earth. Eleven of the accelerators are highlighted red, flashing arrows beside them indicating their rotation and direction. A trajectory forms, joining the eleven accelerators and then plunging into the heart of Saturn. Naki set this up yesterday, the three of them poring over the trajectory together until they were certain there was no room for error. The order came from the Charlemagne, a belt-and-braces test firing to confirm the calibration tests for accelerators four and eight and the integrity of all the communications relays. *That* much, Naki has shared, but not the why. It's unusual. Outside the standard procedures for calibration.

'Artemis is in position. Ready to initiate firing sequence,' Janus informs her.

'Target?' Not that she needs to ask.

'Saturn main planetary mass.'

'Error probability?'

'Estimated probability of impact error is one part in ten thousand and diminishing. Do you wish to manually command this firing, Commander, or to proceed with automatic initiation?'

'Automatic.' Allowing Janus to begin the sequence is preferred procedure. An artificial intelligence will issue commands with a precision of nanoseconds, not the few seconds either way which is more normal for a human operator. Precision sequencing is critical for the Sentinel. Naki, an American Football fan, likens it to having thirty quarterbacks who must all be in exactly the right place when the ball arrives to throw it to the next and the next and the next until finally it reaches a wide receiver in mid-leap, to land with the ball in his hand for an immediate touchdown. It's a crude analogy but it works. If any accelerator is out of position by even a metre when the projectile arrives, the sequence will fail, very likely with the spectacular loss of both accelerator and projectile.

'Automated sequencing confirmed. Firing in three, two, one… Sequence commenced.'

There is no shudder. No boom. Nothing. Somewhere out in space, a million kilometres away, the Artemis drone has nudged a hundred kilograms of space debris into the waiting maw of the primary accelerator. The rock will emerge at a speed of around one million kilometres per second, arrowing towards the second accelerator. And so on and so on until the last flings it at whatever target has become Naki's wide receiver of the day.

She watches the trajectory monitor on the wall. The first red arrow turns green. A white spot begins to move along the plotted path. Most of the accelerators are far outside Saturn's rings, the separation between them millions of kilometres. Nevertheless, at these speeds, the sequence will be swift.

'Accelerator one sequence successful,' Janus informs her.

'Janus, bring up the schematics for the comms array that links us to the accelerators.' Karl's faulty relays still bother her. Two at the same time? She can understand the error, but for both antennas to fail at once seems strange.

The larger image of Saturn, the feed from one of the Sentinel accelerators, rotates until the coloured bands of Saturn's atmosphere fill its field of view. Beside it, a complex matrix of circuit diagrams appears on yet another wall-screen. The white dot on the trajectory plot passes the second red arrow.

'Accelerator two sequence successful.' The rest will happen very quickly now.

Every astronaut learns the basics of electrical engineering, how to read circuit diagrams and engineering schematics. In space, an astronaut is everything: electrician, mechanic, hydraulic engineer, nutritionist, medic, psychologist… but it's one thing being able to read a circuit diagram and entirely another to work out from first principles what sort of fault could render precisely two accelerators out of commission. So instead, as the white spot on the trajectory plot moves ever faster and as Janus rattles through each accelerator, reporting success after success, Roxy records a video query of her own and sends it to ESA Mission Support: Engineering. ESA's first-line support is run from the Charlemagne, and all technical communication between Charlemagne and Saturn is considered classified, which means no QIF piggy-back from the Cronos and thus no quick answer. She supposes it doesn't matter. Most likely, she's only asking the same questions Naki already asked yesterday.

The view of Saturn's atmosphere shakes a little. Something small and bright streaks towards the surface, a momentary line of light and then gone. A fraction of a second later, a tiny flicker blooms and dies as the projectile strikes Saturn's upper atmosphere, burns up and dies.

'Calibration complete,' Janus informs her. 'Commander, we have received the trajectory plan for your return.'

'Put it on the main screen.'

Saturn and its rings disappear. In their place is an evolving time-lapse schematic of the Saturn local system. Saturn and its rings and moons, one bright dot marking Epimetheus, thirty-seven red triangles for the thirty-seven accelerators all moving in their ever-evolving orbits. A new trajectory begins to appear, a series of ever more eccentric ellipses around the planet, starting from Epimetheus, moving through multiple accelerators with every pass around Saturn until finally shooting off the edge of the screen.

'Are you happy, Commander,' asks Janus, 'To be heading home?'

Day Four: 0500 hours

'You were going to tell me why you think they deserve it.' Karl and Roxy sit, bored, in the hub. Roxy is supposed to be asleep but Naki's excursion to the surface has thrown their shifts into disarray. Protocol prefers both other crew members to be awake and present in the hub when the third is suited up and outside in case of emergency. If Naki gets into trouble, one of them will have to suit up and go to help while the other coordinates from the hub.

Naki has been outside for hours, checking in every ten minutes to report that she's still alive and otherwise not saying a word about why she's out there or what she's doing, dutifully keeping to herself whatever classified instructions she's received from Charlemagne. Karl and Roxy, bored and tired, have settled into a game of shots, taking it in turns to slug water from a flask and pretending to get drunk. It's a game every bit as desperate as it sounds, conjured, as they both gleefully admit, from the far edges of ennui.

'They should be locked up!' says Roxy, slurring with abandon. 'They all should be fuckin' executed. All the lunars wanted was

40

some autonomy and the right to govern themselves. I mean, we sat back and let them stay up there for years, what did we expect? More than a decade, some of them! They had fuckin' children, for Christ's sake. On the Moon! Fuckin' children on the Moon! If nothing else, they deserve respect just for that! All they wanted was to stay and do their own thing, same as anyone on Earth. They weren't asking for much, but oh no. We said they were terrorists and we killed them. If that's not a fuckin' war-crime, I don't want to know what is.'

Karl ponders this. He nods profoundly, wagging a pretend-drunk finger repeatedly against the air. 'But they threatened the Earth with a mass driver, right! They blew up the SpaceX station, right! They fired first! What were we supposed to do? Wait until they dropped a rock on Paris? London? Rome?'

Roxy dismisses this with an airy wave. 'SpaceX Station? That plastic piece of folly? Place had been abandoned twenty years! Was floating trash already stripped for parts! Anyway, the only mass drivers on the Moon were built to deliver raw materials into orbit. Fixed site, set up so they *couldn't* throw rocks that would hit the atmosphere and re-enter even if they wanted to! And even if they *could*, so what? Take out the accelerators. Fine. Don't have to wipe out an entire fuckin' colony to do that.'

'I heard they'd been building more.'

'With what materials? Fuckin' false flag knee-jerking fear-mongering bull-fucking-shit of the first order! There's no way they had the resources!' Roxy stops. Hangs her head. Then slowly and carefully pushes the flask of water aside. When she speaks again, she's stone-cold sober. 'Sorry, Karl. I'm not in the right place for this today. Not with Naki outside and… whatever this secret bullshit she's up to.'

41

Karl nods, shrugging off his own drunk act. 'Yeah. Wrong time, huh?'

'I mean it though. It can't be true that no one knew how many people were still up there. So yes, those people, I think they *should* face justice. But they won't, because even though we know it was all a lie, no one can prove it. They'll close ranks, and if one of them looks like they might break, the others will find a way to keep them quiet.' Roxy shivers. 'Sorry, but I know what they're like.'

'You supported the lunars? Bet you kept *that* quiet.'

'No, I didn't support them. Back then I thought the same as everyone else, that it was them or us, because that's what I was told, that we hit them because they were about to do worse. I was *relieved*. Christ, I know people who even cheered. But afterwards, when I saw what we'd done, that we'd hit the colony itself... And the bullshit of the ESA inquiry, that fatuous claim that someone from outside meddled with the systems? I know that place. It's not possible. It was a careful and deliberate lie to hide –'

Roxy stops, frozen to the spot as a series of vibrations tingle her feet. An astronaut spends most of her time holding on to things, in contact with some part of the structure that keeps them alive. Fingers learn what to expect. The constant checking of heat and vibration, like a medic testing a patient's temperature and blood pressure, a matter of habit. And the vibration Roxy has felt isn't a part of the regular thrum of Epimetheus. It is a sharp staccato rattle with no rhythm, like somewhere far away, someone has thrown a handful of gravel at a large tin box. In fact, it is a *lot* like someone has thrown a handful of gravel at a large tin box, and they've the thrown it very hard, and the tin box is the one in which Roxy lives.

She looks to Karl and sees he feels it too. 'Shit!' she hisses. 'I think –'

The first alarm sounds, confirming Roxy's unvoiced guess that Epimetheus has been hit by a meteor shower. She's already moving, Karl too, instinct and training taking over, kicking their way to where three panels have opened in the wall to reveal armoured space suits that Naki likes to joke look like medieval suits of armour. One of the alcoves is already empty, of course, because –

'Naki! Shit!' Roxy's suit is turned away, the back wide open; as she steps into it, it seals itself behind her.

'You in?' Karl's voice is a tinny thing now, coming from beside her ear.

'I'm armoured. You?'

'I'm good. Don't know yet if this was a hit or a near miss.'

'Naki!'

'I know.'

Roxy waits, which right now is all she can do. The armoured suit is inside an armoured alcove in the hub, which itself is at the heart of the station. Wrapped around the hub are the social club, the exercise room and the personal private spaces for the three crew. Below are the critical life support systems, the air and water recyclers. The rest of Epimetheus station is built around these rooms like a cocoon. Mostly, though, what's keeping her safe is a hundred metres of rock and ice between her and the surface.

But not Naki. Naki has no protection at all except her suit, which is as good as nothing, and blind dumb luck.

'Naki!' Every instinct is to call the major on the radio, reach out to her and find out if she's okay; but instinct isn't the same as protocol, and protocol says that Naki, on the surface, doesn't need the distraction of helpless crew members who can't do anything useful bleating on at her for their own peace of mind. There's nothing either of them can do. Janus will become Naki's guide; and if something *does* go wrong up there, it's Janus that Naki's suit will tell.

'Sit tight until the alarm stops,' says Karl. 'All we can do is ride this out.' A meteor strike might mean nothing. It might mean repairing a few of the surface antennas. Probably nothing more. At worst, it *might* mean an evacuation, which makes it fortunate that the Cronos is here.

Roxy tries to imagine what it must be like to be on the surface right now and finds she can't. 'Mansplaining the safety procedures to me isn't helping my stress levels.' For now, everything is centred around keeping her and Karl safe; so she'll follow procedure and stay exactly where she is until the shower is over and Janus has estimated the damage.

If Janus is still there, of course.

'Yeah. And I'm following them by keeping us talking and making sure we still have comms.'

'I'm not about to panic, Karl.' Janus has triggered countless drills over the years. This is the third time it's been real. The other times, there was no damage. Something struck Epimetheus, but not any part that mattered. Likely as not, this will be the same.

The other times, they didn't have an astronaut on the surface.

'How was the rest of your conversation with the Cronos?'

'Pleasant enough.'

'Who'd you talk to?'

'Karl!'

'Who?'

'Doctor Rakhi Chandrasekar.'

'I got a Flight Lieutenant Kris Bradford. I mean, they could have had me talk to the ship's artificial intelligence and not bothered with a human being at all, I suppose. What did you talk about?'

'Seriously?' Understanding what Karl's doing doesn't make it less irritating.

'Seriously, Rox. *You* might not be about to panic but I'm shitting myself here. They had some issue with their AI, I think. My guy was as tight as a fist around a rich man's windpipe. You hear anything about that?'

'No. They tell you I'm leaving early?' Protocol says to wait in their armoured alcoves, no matter what, until the alarm stops. Karl is giving her mind something to do beyond screaming at her to move. It hadn't occurred to her that perhaps he feels the same.

She hears his wariness. 'Yeah. They mentioned that.'

'They tell you how?'

'No.'

'They tell you why?'

'I figured they need you aboard for something.'

'Really? Like what? You've seen the crew manifest. What special skills do I bring that they don't already have covered?'

'It was either that or because you're a general's daughter.' He tries to make it sound like a joke but can't quite hide the spike of truth. It *is* what he thought.

'They're not transferring me to the Cronos. My mother wants to use our accelerators to hurl astronauts between worlds and I'm her guinea pig. They're going to fire me back to Earth. I'll be home in three months. Whether I arrive alive and angry or smeared into meat paste depends on whether someone somewhere made a mistake with their maths, and given ESA's history... Well, you can see how I might have concerns.'

The alarm abruptly stops. Silence hangs between them.

'Janus?'

'Commanders, the danger appears to have passed. Life support remains uncompromised. Integrity of the pressurised compartments of the station remains at a hundred percent.'

'And Naki?' Roxy is already emerging from her alcove. Across the hub, Karl is doing the same.

'Unfortunately, I am unable to contact Major Nakita.'

'Her suit?'

'I am receiving no response.'

'Shit!' Roxy opens a channel of her own, knowing as she does that it's pointless but doing it anyway. 'Naki? Major Nakita! Respond, please, if you can!' If Naki could hear and was able to reply, Janus would have said so. 'Karl, I'm going after her.'

She expects resistance, a mixture of Karl's latent sexism and the very real truth that neither of them knows what she'll be walking into up there and that Karl is unquestionably more comfortable going outside than either Roxy or Naki.

Their protocols say to wait, even under circumstances such as these. But set against that is the sure knowledge that if Naki is in trouble on the surface, every second counts.

Karl only hesitates a moment. 'Agreed. I'll keep everything here nailed down. I've got your back.'

Roxy is already on her way out.

'Rox?'

'Suit pings every thirty seconds. Yes, Yes, I know.'

'No. Open channel. Keep talking. And Rox... Stay safe. Whatever state Naki's in, we need two functioning crew members or Janus shuts us down and Sentinel goes off-line.'

'That's cold, Karl.' Roxy reaches the airlock. On the far side, the elevator to the surface is still working, which is good news; although in the micro-gravity of Epimetheus, an ascent of a hundred metres is more of an annoyance than a real obstacle.

'Sorry. I'm scared, okay. You and Naki are my friends and I like you both and I don't want to be trapped out here all on my own. Better?'

'Better.' The airlock cycles. As it the outer door opens, the elevator to the surface arrives, ready and waiting. 'Still nothing from Naki?'

'No. Getting a pile of other faults, though, all comms stuff. The primary Earth-transmission antenna is responsive but reporting multiple failures. The accelerator arrays are operational. Artemis is still on its way back from Naki's calibration sequence but I'm getting no response to a request to run a self-test. That's probably the comms link rather than Artemis herself. Naki was checking the accelerator arrays when the shower hit, right?'

'Right.' The elevator's ascent speed of one metre per second feels absurdly slow.

'Right. So those are all still working. So that's not where it hit, so maybe she's okay and it's just a comms thing.'

Naki isn't okay and it isn't just comms thing. That's not how these things go.

'Janus, send one drone to Major Nakita's last reported position, one to the Artemis antenna and one to the Earth transmission antenna.' The three remote drones are intended for exactly this, for surveying the surface, for inspecting the aftermath of the occasional meteor strike, for damage assessment and anything where a remote visual inspection will spare someone an excursion out of the sanctuary of the hub.

'Other systems are within usual functional parameters. As far as I can tell, it's just the Earth transmitter and the link to Artemis.'

Without Artemis, Janus can't position a projectile at the first accelerator, which makes them useless. Without the transmit antenna, their link to earth has become one-way. Right now, Epimetheus can receive a firing order but can't execute it and can't report back to Earth.

None of which is as bad as losing one of their crew.

'Rox?'

'What?'

'You've gone quiet.'

'Sorry. Almost at the surface now. We can still talk to Earth through the Cronos, right?'

'As far as I know.'

The elevator starts to slow. 'Talk to them.'

'I can't tell them we're out of action.'

'Not directly, but you can get them to set up a link to Charlemagne and send an encrypted burst, right? Let them know we're out of action for a while and ask them what they want us to do.'

'I'm on it.'

The Cronos shows up, and then all this? Can't be a coincidence. 'Karl... Be careful what you say when you talk to the Cronos.'

'You want to womansplain the security protocols some more?'

'Ha ha. Right, I'm reaching the surface now.'

The elevator stops with the tiniest jolt, still enough to send Roxy floating off her feet before Epimetheus's feeble gravity grabs her back. She tethers her suit as the doors open, then turns to face the surface. She needs a moment, bracing herself for this. For standing on a tiny piece of rock, in a fast close orbit about the girded colossus overhead. Saturn, vast, on the horizon, filling a quarter of the sky. The shimmering line of its rings. The millions upon millions of stars. All the same view as she sees every day on the screens in the hub and in her room, but out here, naked under the stars…

Chandrasekhar was right, she thinks. You can never get used to this. Not *this*.

'Got you on visual. Surface camera three.' The moment is broken.

'Janus, give me Major Nakita's last known position.' Roxy flips a switch on the back of her glove and a HUD overlay appears on her visor, a map of the surface site of Epimetheus station.

'I'm sorry, Commander, but that information is classified.'

'You get that, Karl?'

'Yup. I get the same answer.'

'What the fuck?'

'No idea.'

With a grunt of exasperation, Roxy steps out. In the distance, straight ahead of her, is the Earth transmit antenna. Even from here, she can see pieces of metal hanging askew where something has punched through. Far away to the left is the receive antenna. Somewhere to the right is the Artemis transmission site, too small at this range to tell whether it's damaged.

'You getting this?' Roxy has Janus show the reported locations of Naki's suit, right up until the meteor shower hit. These have her moving between the accelerator arrays, pausing at the antennas for accelerators four and eight, the first for thirty minutes, the second for only half that time. Then she starts back and seems to freeze. The freeze is a full hour ago, which Roxy takes to be the time at which Naki decided to mask where she was and what she was doing.

The drone at Naki's last position shows nothing. Not even footprints, because the surface of Epimetheus is ice and rock, not dust like the Moon.

'I'm seeing it.'

The Artemis transmit station is a ruin. The whole area is peppered with craters, each a few metres across. The array has taken a hit, reducing it to mangled garbage. There's no salvaging to be done here.

'We'll have to replace the Artemis station.' They have the parts for that. The earth transmit array, if it's in the same state, will be another matter.

For a moment, Karl doesn't answer. When he does, his voice is flat.

'I found the major,' he says.

Drone pictures stream to Roxy's HUD. There are two gaping holes punched through the frame of the Earth transmit antenna. The bulk of the structure appears to be intact, although only a closer inspection will reveal the true extent of the damage. About a dozen metres from the antenna, the drone is looking at a figure lying prone on the ice. A figure that can only by Major Nakita.

Roxy stifles a gasp, half shock, half regret. 'I'm going to bring her in.'

It's extremely unlikely that Naki is still alive if her suit has died, but it's not impossible, and so Roxy sets off, careful jets propelling her in huge leaps across the surface, eyes focussed on the ground. It's too easy, out here, to make a mistake. The gravity on Epimetheus is feeble, the monstrous bulk of Saturn so close that one misplaced burst could launch her out of Epimetheus's reach and into orbit around Saturn itself. Slow are careful is the only way, which is why she's still outside when her HUD lights up again. A personal message, through the still-working Earth Receive Array from General Micah.

'Commander, please be informed that the ICC verdict will be announced tomorrow. We need to talk before that happens. Use the Cronos QIF but be advised that we may be obliged to switch to a secure channel. Please respond as soon as possible.'

As soon as possible will have to wait. Roxy bounds on, towards the ruined antenna and her dead commanding officer and friend. Light gleams across Saturn's rings, cold and majestic.

Day Four: 1400 hours

Aside from her helmet, Roxy is still suited when she walks back into the hub. Her magnetic boots click-clack as she walks across the room, clumsy, uncertain of quite how to do the whole walking thing in near-zero gravity, or why she should even bother, yet reluctant to let it go.

'Karl?' She starts to shed the suit, a clumsy and awkward process, not well-practiced. She doesn't go outside very often. Mostly, she simply sits in this room, talking to Karl and Naki because there's no one else. They read a lot, sometimes to each other, sometimes not. They watch a lot of movies, sometimes together, sometimes alone.

She won't be talking to Naki again. Major Nakita is dead. She's still in her suit, laid out in one of the workshops where she and Karl will have to assemble a new jury-rigged array to talk to the Artemis drone and, if they can, repair the damaged panels of the Earth Transmit Antenna. The pain of leaving Naki suited is almost a physical thing, but they simply don't have the resources to do more, not now, not yet. They are two astronauts, alone and far from home, with no way to contact Earth. The damage to

Naki is obvious. Struck in the back by a meteorite. She must have been hunched over something; the entry point is between her shoulders, destroying most of the suit systems and rupturing both air tanks, but that isn't what killed her. What killed her was how the meteor – and perhaps fragments of the ruined suit itself – passed right through Naki herself, pulverising her from sternum to pelvis.

She tries not to think about this and fails. It would have been quick, at least. Most likely, Naki never knew what happened.

'Karl! Are you there? Where are you?' She frees her arms and shoulders from the suit.

'Commander Veers is in his quarters. I instructed him to rest as soon as you were safely inside the elevator,' Janus tells her.

'He's asleep?' A part of her rails at this, because how can he sleep at a time like this? But at the same time, the part of her that's a professional astronaut understands. They have work to do, and tired astronauts make mistakes, and mistakes are fatal. And Karl probably *isn't* asleep, much as he might want to be.

'Okay, Janus. I need you to prepare another encrypted message to relay to Charlemagne via the Cronos and then open a channel for me to speak with them. Message to Charlemagne is this: Epimetheus suffered meteor impacts while Makor Nakita was on an excursion following instructions from Charlemagne. Damage sustained to both the Earth Transmit Antenna and the Artemis Array. Both out of commission. We have three holes the size of dinner plates through our Earth Transmit Antenna. It looks repairable but it'll take a day or two and will require at least two further excursions to detach the damaged sections, bring them inside, effect repairs, and take them out again. Until these repairs are done, we're going to be relying on the Cronos to talk to Earth. Epimetheus remains capable of receiving direct communication. The Artemis array looks like god punched it in the face. It's not repairable. Epimetheus proposes to replace the array using parts available on-station. Please advise.' She pulls herself free of the suit and drifts to the chair, grabs it, straps herself in, and bashes the side of the still-blank screen. 'All other systems appear intact. Life support integrity has not been compromised. However, Makor Nakita did not survive the incident. Believe death was instant. Please advise. Message ends.'

Exasperated, she takes a moment to compose herself.

'Can you piggy-back that onto an open transmission to Charlemagne while I talk to them via the Cronos?'

'Yes, Commander. Commander Veers has already established a protocol… Commander, I have the Cronos for you.'

Chandrasekhar's face appears on the screen. She looks anxious. 'Doctor, thank you for –'

'Rakhi. Please. We've been trying to reach you for hours. You broadcast an emergency distress warning. Is everything okay? You look –'

'Epimetheus rode a meteor shower a few hours back. We've been busy.' What she wants to say, is that they're down Earth-comms, can't talk to their Artemis and have a dead crew member, that they've just become a super-expensive observatory-cum-psychology experiment; but all of that is classified and, broadcast to the universe at large, could see her court-martialled.

Does she care? It's hard to worry about something so small at a time like this.

Wait… 'You've been trying to reach us for all this time? You never spoke to Commander Veers?'

Rakhi frowns. 'Not that I am aware.'

'Sorry. It *is* a bad time, but it's nothing serious and we're no longer in any danger. We'll have everything back working again in a few hours and have no need of your assistance.' The words sound feeble and unbelievable. 'Charlemagne has requested I contact them via QIF as soon as possible. Would you be able to arrange that?'

'Of course. Is this an official matter?' A faint effort of a smile, but Roxy hears a crack in Chandrasekhar's voice. Should she read anything into that, and into Rakhi's question? Do they already know more? It's possible, after all, that they have telescopes of their own, powerful enough to see the damage to Epimetheus.

'It's personal. My mother is on Charlemagne. Charlemagne is aware we're suffered an incident. I think she just wants some face time to make sure I'm okay.' To Roxy, the lie sounds preposterous.

'I will pass the request to Captain Zeedorf immediately.'

'Thank you.'

'Commander... Roxy... I... shouldn't say this, but Captain Zeedorf may not be able to oblige you.' Rakhi smiles and nods and almost laughs as she says this but there's something else in her eyes, something anxious.

Something she isn't saying. 'Is everything okay over there?'

'We are having difficulties with our communications array. It's probably nothing.' She purses her lips. 'Your capsule was deployed five hours ago and will reach you in another fifteen. It may be... prudent for you to take over control of the terminal phase of the flight.'

The capsule for her return to Earth. She'd forgotten. Presumably, the plan is now null and void. With Naki gone, she'll have to stay. Janus won't allow the station to operate with only one crew member. Her mother might have been willing to pull her out early, leaving Karl and Naki alone, leaving Epimetheus short-handed until the *Voyager* arrives, but ESA won't allow

Epimetheus to go off-line completely, not even for General Micah.

'Roxy?'

Her mind is racing, spinning off the rails. It's too much to process all at once. She forces herself to focus. First things first, get the Earth Transmit Antenna working again. Then she can talk to the Charlemagne while she and Karl fix the link to Artemis. Find out what Charlemagne wants them to do now Naki's gone.

'Sorry. Distracted.'

'I hope we will speak again before you leave.'

Roxy frowns. The words are spoken as though by someone who thinks that perhaps they won't.

'Thank you. Rakhi… ESA protocols require me to inform you that Epimetheus possesses sufficient capacity to offer indefinite recycled air and water life support for up to four people and can provide emergency support for up to seven for a period of six months.' No such ESA protocol exists, as far as Roxy is aware, but it eases Roxy's mind to offer a lifeline, faint and almost certainly useless as it is. She's not sure why, exactly, but the way Chandrasekhar speaks reeks of anxiety.

'Six months is enough to last until the *Voyager* arrives,' she adds.

'I will pass this along to Captain Zeedorf. Goodbye. And good luck.'

Chandrasekhar ends the link, and the finality in these words does nothing to ease Roxy's thoughts.

There is work to be done. Roxy instructs Janus to send the message to Charlemagne as soon as the Cronos QIF link is established, if it ever is, and settles to planning their next few shifts. The first issue will be the Earth Transmit Array. When Karl comes off his sleep cycle, one of them will have to go to fetch the damaged sections of the antenna while the other works on the replacement Artemis array. They'll work on the repairs together after that, making communications with Earth their priority. It'll take at least three more excursions to the surface. It would be quicker and easier if they worked on everything together, but Janus will demand that both of them stay awake through each excursion, which means they'll have to take turns on the repairs while the other sleeps.

Or tries to.

Day 5: 0300 hours

It's Karl who proposes the plan. They might have drawn straws for it, but Roxy sees no reason to argue. She was the one who went outside to retrieve Naki, after all. She saw the damage first-hand. It makes sense for her to be the one to go back and bring back the damaged panels. While she works, Karl will track her progress and work on the replacement base station for the Artemis drone. When she returns, they'll finish the work inside and maybe start on the antenna panels. Then they'll both rest, and Janus can run the station alone, and screw protocol. Tomorrow, Roxy will work on the antenna panels while Karl takes the new Artemis Array outside and sets it to work. Then they'll swap places. Roxy will replace the damaged antenna panels. By the end of another day, Epimetheus will be operational again. They'll both sleep, and upset Janus again, and maybe have a drink to celebrate their success. Then, finally, they'll mourn for Naki; but for now, in unspoken agreement, they don't talk about her. Instead, Roxy is telling Karl about the capsule from the Cronos as she suits up, and how her mother planned to bring her home. All of which is irrelevant with Naki gone, but they talk as though it still might happen.

'Hey. I'll still be waiting with a cold one for you when you get back. Promise.'

Karl shakes this off. He's listened to Charlemagne's plan and isn't impressed. 'Have they trialled this?'

'Thousands of times, in simulation. It makes sense. You want to spend three years in cold sleep when it could be three months?'

'Jesus! But… So… *How?*'

'They limit the accelerations to a survivable level and push me into an orbit around Saturn.' Roxy runs through the safety checks on her suit as she talks, Karl double-checking everything she does. 'They have a trajectory that uses all the accelerators to fling me at Earth. At the other end, NEADRA does the same, only in reverse. Three to four months and I'm in orbit around Earth. Unless the capture fails, of course.' She snorts.

'Have they tested this for real? No, they haven't, have they? And we both know it, because if they had, *we'd* be the ones running the tests!'

Roxy shrugs. 'Unless there's something you're not telling me.'

'It's not funny. This pod? They could have fired it from Earth in the same way. Had us catch it. Tested the whole procedure for real. They could have done that, at least! Make sure it arrives.'

They stare at each other. Until now, Roxy had never considered this. Now that she does, she had to concede that Karl has a point. But that's not the only thing. She lets out a long breath. 'The Cronos left three years ago. They had to have been planning this long before. That makes it before either of us even got here.'

'Yeah. They've planned this for that long and they didn't tell us.'

'Me, Karl. They didn't tell *me*. The Cronos only has one pod.'

'I stay stuck out here, do I?'

'Think of the money. And of not being a test subject in an experiment that could leave you adrift in space or smeared into mince.'

Karl snorts. 'Nice image, Rox. They must *really* want you back on Earth.'

'Happy to swap. I suppose they'll be planning on sending future relief crews out the same way. If it works, the *Voyager* could be the last ship to come out here.'

Karl hands Roxy her helmet. 'Yeah.' He stares at her, as if wrestling with something. 'Rox… We've been company for each other for the best part of three years. For most of that time, you've been the only other human around. I always knew you came out here for a reason. I knew you from the start you were running from something and obviously I have a fair idea what it is. But I never asked because I figured you'd tell me whatever you wanted me to know. Your mother murdered the Moon. But that wasn't *you*, Rox. That's on her, and you know that, and you're not stupid or fragile or weak, so there's more to this. I'm just saying that I'm here. If you want to talk, that is. Sometimes it helps to get it out. You won't find a better place to leave a secret behind you.'

'I'm not the only running from something, Karl.'

'No. You're not.'

'So what? I show you mine and you show me yours? Is that the idea?'

Karl shakes his head. 'I'll tell my story either way if you want to hear it. I was going to wait until you were on your way home.

You'll understand why when you hear what it is. Let's get this mess sorted first though, eh?'

Roxy weighs this up. It takes a moment before she reaches a decision. But yes, some things *are* better out than in, and the last time anyone went outside, someone died, and if that's going to happen she wants this out of her before she goes. 'You've been watching the trial, right?' Stupid question. They all have.

'Along with the whole rest of humanity, I suspect.'

'The whole chain of command is on trial. Top to bottom. All the media attention is on the United Nations Security Council and the President and General Committee of the Agency. Was President Serpicha permitted to give the order to NEADRA without getting it sanctioned by the Council of Europe first? That sort of thing. But the NEADRA staff officers know they're on trial too, right down to the ones who carried the orders.'

Karl nods. 'Sure. The whole chain of command. Was the order lawful? Should it have been obeyed? All that shit. Does it matter? Maybe Serpicha's order was a war crime or maybe it wasn't. After that, everyone simply did what they were told, like they were supposed to. They'll all be found innocent. If they find anyone guilty, it'll be Serpicha, since it doesn't matter, what with him being dead.'

'Do you think that's right?'

'Does it matter what I think?'

'You're the only other human I know for a billion kilometres. Yes, it matters. To me, at least.'

Karl lets out a long heavy breath. 'You honestly want to know?'

'Karl!'

'All right. It *was* a war crime, but you can't lay it just on Serpicha. The order had to go through the chiefs of staff to get to

NEADRA. Every head of state in Europe must have known, and not just there, either. The Americans, the Russians, the Chinese, the Indians, the Japanese, anyone with a presence in Earth orbit, any of them could have stopped it. The whole system is guilty. What I think is that anyone who knew the risk of what they were doing, following orders or not, should be shot.' He chuckles, although there's nothing funny here. 'You get posted to this place, I guess it's impossible not to have a good long think about what happened on Tranquillity. I'm guessing that's not what you wanted to hear.'

There's a long silence before Roxy replies. 'Everyone knows my mother was in command that night. The order came to her. If anyone should have turned around and said no, she was the one to do it. But she didn't. What you probably don't know is that there *were* people who refused. She had them relieved. She followed through, too, had them court-martialled for dereliction even after we all knew what we'd done. I've never seen the slightest glimmer of remorse or shame.' She shivers. 'She talked to me a couple of days ago. I think she already knows she's safe.'

Karl shrugs. 'It's all or nothing. Too many powerful people with too much at stake. The wrong verdict would bring everything down and so nothing will happen.'

'Yes. And when I get back to Earth, she'll be waiting. She probably won't be the first person I'll see, but she won't be far behind. She'll salute and expect me to salute back, and call her Ma'am, and take her orders. She truly believes we did nothing wrong. I don't know how to live with that.' Roxy stops. Takes a few deep breaths, looking to gather her composure. Karl remains silent, no emotion at all on his face. Waiting for more, perhaps. 'Can I ask you something?'

Karl nods.

'If you'd been there that night, would you have risked your career, your livelihood, your future, to try and stop it? If you'd truly believed Tranquillity was about to launch rocks that would slash through the atmosphere, that each one would hit the surface of the Earth with the force of a nuke, that every strike might mean tens of thousands of dead? Knowing that if it started, they could fire fifty or sixty times before being silenced?'

'You mean if I really, honestly believed all that crap, and had no idea that there were families and they were desperate?' Karl shakes his head. 'I don't know, Rox. I'd like to think so. But probably not.'

'What if it had been down to you to actually press the button?'

This gets her a faint smile. 'It's hard, Rox, trying to imagine a thing like that, pretending I don't know what the consequences were.'

Roxy tried to let this sink in. Tries to let herself see it through those eyes, but it's no good. 'The trial was supposed to –'

'Would *you* press the button?'

'No!' Roxy's answer is sharp and immediate, almost violent. 'No, I wouldn't.'

'Even if it meant a court-martial?'

'Even if it meant far worse. I couldn't.'

The last words hang in the air. For a long time, there seems to be nothing else.

'I guess they chose the right girl to send out here, then,' Karl says. He sounds quiet and sad, like something has changed between them. 'Go get this done. I'll be watching while I work on the Artemis Array. We can talk more when you get back if you want. And you *will* come back, right? No stupid mistakes out there.'

Roxy doesn't move. For a long time, it seems she barely even breathes. Then she puts the suit helmet over her head and locks it in place and double-checks the seals. A long, tedious and exhausting job is exactly what she needs to occupy her mind. Something to give her thoughts a place to dwell other than Naki, and the past, and what she did. The inevitable cause and effect that have brought her here.

Day 6: 0100 hours

Roxy sits in the command hub. An hour ago, she finished work on repairing the antenna panels. As far she was able to tell on yesterday's excursion, the Earth Transmit base station is still functional. The repaired antenna panels are sitting in the workshop, next to Naki's body. Naki is still in her armoured suit but wrapped in foil now. Naki being there is why Roxy is in the hub, not the workshop.

They haven't slept. Either of them. Janus is bleating about protocols but fuck that. Right now, Karl is outside. He's been out for hours, setting up the new Artemis base station. As soon as he gets back, Roxy will go out and make the repairs to the antenna. If all goes well, they'll get a message to Earth. Then they'll sleep.

She reviews the comms logs. Something to do. The messages from Charlemagne indicate her burst via the Cronos got through. Earth knows what happened, which is a relief. They have detailed instructions for the antenna repair, which she and Karl have followed to the letter. Instructions, too, for what to do with Major Nakita's body which, for the moment, they haven't. There's no way to get her back to Earth. Burial in space, drifting forever in orbit around Saturn, a tiny new moon. But that can wait. When the repairs are done, they'll give Naki a proper send-off. And then, at last, maybe she can rest.

The giant wall-screen shows news from Earth. A reporter stands in front of the International Criminal Court in The Hague. Around the entrance, the previous gathering of protesters has grown into a crowd, rowdy but otherwise peaceful, held back by a cordon of police. Their placards call for justice for the Sea of Tranquillity massacre. An empty lectern, crowded with microphones, stands at the top of the steps by the doors. Around the fringes of the crowd are more reporters and television crews. As Roxy watches, the court doors open. A woman and two men walk out, all wearing the black and blue robes and white cravats that mark them as judges. A dozen security personnel flank them. The noise from the crowd rises, then falls as the lead judge steps to the lectern. The screen above the doors rolls down behind her, covering them. On it is projected a picture of the Moon.

It's finally happening. A verdict on what her mother did.

The image on Roxy's screen changes to a close-up of the presiding judge, standing at the lectern.

'In 2065, the inhabitants of the Sea of Tranquillity declared their independence from Earth, demanding a substantial increase in the deliveries of essential materials in exchange for continued supply of lunar resources to Earth orbit. This trial has heard from survivors about the conditions of working in the Sea of Tranquillity, and from representatives of the nation states and corporate sponsors who invested in the construction of the lunar mines and vehemently opposed any such agreement. It is largely a matter of public record how those talks eventually broke down. To the rest of the world, this was a simple trade dispute, one that received little attention until NASA and the European and Chinese Space Agencies declared an embargo on supply missions to the Moon.'

The image behind the judge changes to that of a spaceship that looks like a space-station with a few rockets hastily bolted on the back. Which is, as Roxy remembers it, largely what it was.

Most of us will remember the Sullenburg, scavenged from sections of the old International Space Station and converted into an evacuation mission to bring the Sea of Tranquillity inhabitants back to Earth. It is again a matter of public record that the Sullenburg successfully evacuated just over half the population and that the other half refused to leave. We have heard from ESA and NASA representatives how the remaining lunar inhabitants were expected to capitulate within weeks as their stores of water, air and food were depleted. We have heard from the surviving Sullenburg evacuees how, while the Sea of Tranquillity facilities were far from self-sufficient, the inhabitants had been stockpiling supplies for at least a year before the initial declaration, and thus why this expectation of quick capitulation was not met.'

'Roxy?' Janus interrupts, speaking over the transmission from Earth.

'Yes?'

'I have been collaborating with the Cronos to guide your return capsule to the station. It will be arriving shortly. Guidance collaboration has ceased. I require your permission to take over terminal guidance.'

'It is also a well-documented that, as the blockade continued, popular opinion on Earth turned against it; until May 17th 2068, when an unknown space object travelling at extreme speed grazed Earth's atmosphere, destroying the uninhabited SpaceX station, the resulting orbital debris causing damage to more than a dozen other satellites. Within days, both ESA and NASA released statements claiming to have back-traced the object's trajectory to the lunar mass drivers on the Sea of Tranquillity.'

'Permission granted.' Roxy is barely listening. The capsule from the Cronos hardly matters now. She won't be leaving any time soon. For once, her mother won't get what she wants.

'It is a further matter of public record that the Sea of Tranquillity issued a statement claiming responsibility for the strike and promising more to come if their demands weren't met. We have seen evidence of the modelling processes and of the underlying data on which the NASA and ESA claims were based. We have heard evidence from Sullenburg evacuees claiming to have been in contact with the Sea of Tranquillity and stating that no such statement was ever issued and claiming the entire event was fabricated to sway opinion on Earth in favour of the blockade. It is critical, at this stage, to note that no evidence beyond personal testimony has been received by this court to substantiate these claims. Nevertheless, we do not dismiss them, nor infer them to be in any way of less weight.'

There. Right there, in those words, Roxy knows what's coming. *No, no, we took everything the Sullenburg evacuees said as seriously as you can imagine. We gave it all the weight we possibly could, but in the end it wasn't enough.* But then, wasn't that always the way this was going to go?

She frowns, lost in thought. Something about the request from Janus nags at her.

'The court has reviewed the order of the United Nations Security Council, issued to the European Space Agency, to formulate a plan to disable the lunar mass drivers. We have heard evidence from advisors and senior executives from corporate and state entities, a full list of which is available along with the transcripts of their testimonies.'

'Janus? Why have we stopped guidance collaboration?' Chandrasekar's farewell tugs at her. *Good luck.* As if she knew something bad was coming.

'Commander, I have lost contact with the Cronos.'

The image behind the judge changes again, now to a low-orbit shot of the Sea of Tranquillity. The domes are mostly replaced by two craters. Those that survive are misshapen, or have gaping holes, or are clearly cracked. The long rectangular accelerators have vanished entirely, fresh craters in their place.

'What do you mean, lost?'

Behind the judge, a series of stills of protest marches and crowds outside landmark buildings across the world, then fixing on a still image of an old and semi-derelict space station.

'All transmissions from the Cronos have ceased.'

'On May 21st, 2068, at 11:35pm Paris Time, the ESA Near-Earth Asteroid Deflection Railgun Array, NEADRA fired a sequence of nine projectiles.'

'They were having trouble with their antenna,' she says, distracted. This trial... she needs to hear it. The verdict. The inevitable damnation of it.

'At 11:57pm, Paris Time, the first of these struck the lunar surface close to Dome Three of the Sea of Tranquillity facility.'

'Wait... *All* transmissions? Including their beacon?'

'Yes, Commander.'

'At 12:01am on May 22nd, a second projectile struck Dome Seven. At 12:05, a third projectile struck Dome Four. The remaining six struck the three lunar mass driver sites. Each projectile was approximately one thousand kilograms in mass, travelling at approximately one tenth of one percent of the speed of light, with an impact energy roughly equivalent to a twenty-kiloton warhead. The effect, as seen in pictures taken some days after the event, was the near-total annihilation of the Sea of Tranquillity facility...'

Roxy sits very still. Trouble with antennas is one thing. But a beacon is a beacon. An entirely separate thing. No beacon means...

'...As far as this court is aware, no transmissions of any sort were made from the surface of the Moon after 11:57pm on May 21st 2068...'

No ship.

'You're sure. No beacon? Did something happen?'

'*...Following the strike, the Sullenburg returned to the Moon and attempted to locate survivors. The court has heard the testimony of nine of the ESA astronauts who conducted this mission and has reviewed extensive footage provided. There were no such survivors...*'

'Unclear. I have been detecting near-continuous transmissions on multiple different frequencies for the last day. They have all stopped.'

'All at once?'

'Yes.'

'*...The aims of the court in this investigation are four-fold. Firstly, to determine whether the remaining inhabitants of the Sea of Tranquillity following the Sullenburg evacuation legally constituted military combatants. Secondly, and following from the first, to determine whether the Sea of Tranquillity facility constituted a legal military target...*'

Roxy tries to imagine how something like this can happen and finds only one answer. The Cronos has gone. Even a complete failure of the ship's power plant wouldn't silence its beacon. She can't imagine anything that would, short of something catastrophic. Detonation of the plasma engines, for example, although such a failure should be almost impossible. Struck by one of the larger pieces of debris that make up Saturn's rings, perhaps? Either way, there should be an explosion. Some flash of light that her long-range imagers, constantly searching the solar system for wandering comets, should detect.

'Was there an explosion?' asks Roxy, because surely there was. 'Is there debris? Were there any survivors?' She tries to imagine it. For the Cronos to go so suddenly silent, she must have been shattered.

'Unclear.'

Unless they went dark by choice? But that makes no sense at all.

'...In more simple terms, were the facilities themselves, excluding the mass drivers, legitimate targets. Thirdly, and following from the second, precisely what order was issued to the ESA NEADRA command, and following what chain of authority. Fourthly, and likewise following from the first and second, was the order issued to NEADRA legal and was it correctly executed.'

There is a pause as the judge gathers herself. The waiting crowd is silent.

'We have line of sight, don't we? She wasn't in Saturn's shadow?'

'The Cronos was detectable to my optical array at the time it ceased transmission. All detections of the Cronos ended simultaneously, across all spectra. I detected an extremely powerful burst of low wavelength radio waves.'

'You're saying it just... vanished?' The screen behind the judge changes again, now displaying the arms of the International Criminal Court.

'Yes, Commander.'

'I will address the first and second of these points together. It is the finding of this court that, while the lunar mass driver complex may have been legally designated a military target, that is not the case for the remainder of the facility. It is our finding that the lunar mass drivers presented the only conceivable threat to life and were sufficiently removed from the remainder of the facility to be considered independent.'

'How far away are they?'

'At the point I was last able to detect their transmissions, approximately one million kilometres.'

Roxy closes her eyes. There will be no rescue, even if there were survivors. The Artemis drone could probably fly that far, eventually, and stay within range of Janus's control, but it would take days. Weeks, even. She doesn't know. At the moment, they can't even talk to it.

She thinks about Karl, out there on the surface. She wants to tell him. Talk to him. But he's outside, in the middle of testing the new Artemis Array. He needs to focus on the task in hand. Until he's done, this one's on her alone.

This finding renders the first question moot: it does not matter whether the remaining lunar population following the Sullenburg evacuation can or cannot be legally classified as combatants: the only legitimate lunar target, under any circumstances, were the mass drivers themselves. Thus it is the finding of this court that the actions taken by NEADRA on the night of May 21st, 2068 were not legal. In layman's terms, whether the lunars fired first or not, the actions of the European Space Agency are classifiable as a war-crime.'

There comes long pause as the words sink in. Cheers from the protestors within the crowd. Roxy stares, dumbstruck, at the screen. This isn't what she expected. It's what's right, to her way of seeing the world, but she's a military girl from a military family. Above all else, the military knows how to close ranks – they coined the phrase, after all. A part of her wants to whoop with joy but she can't, not now, not with Naki dead in the workshop above her head and now the disappearance of the Cronos.

'Assuming whatever's left is still in the same orbit, how long for a drone to get there?'

'Based on predictions of its previous orbit and assuming that communications can be re-established, seventy-one hours. However, if the Cronos was struck by an object, the impact will have changed the orbits of both. In the time it would take any drone to arrive, the surviving mass would have deviated significantly from its previous trajectory. It is not possible to compute an intercept.'

'It's gone, then.' And if anyone survived, they have nothing to look forward to but a cold and lonely death as their oxygen drains. As lonely as it's humanly possible to be.

The thought still nags at her: *Unless she went dark by choice.*

She sends a call to Karl. 'Check in, Veers.'

'Still here.' Karl sounds calm and assured. 'Just got a few more tests to run. Looks good so far. You watching the trial?'

'Don't tell me *you* are?'

'I see the verdict's coming.'

'Fuck's sake! Mind on the job, Karl!'

'Don't worry. I'm focussed.'

She can't tell him about the Cronos. Not now. Not until he's back inside. She almost tries to open a channel to Earth before she remembers that she can't; and even if she could, without the Cronos as an intermediary, not without a one-hour delay each way.

Nothing to do but wait, and so that's what she does, watching the screen as the final scenes of the final act unfold of a story that started almost a decade ago. This, too, is an hour behind. Over on the Cronos, with their magical QIF antenna, they already knew how it ended before they disappeared. They were seeing all this an hour ahead of her.

And then they simply disappear? Can that be coincidence?

The judge at her lectern begins again as the hoots and jeers and cheers of the crowd die down. *I will now move to the remaining points to be ruled on by this court. In the evidence submitted to us, it is not disputed that the United Nations Security Council authorised the European Space Agency to determine a plan for rendering the lunar mass drivers ineffective by use of the NEADRA. In testimony to us, the European Space Agency has stated that contingency preparations were made for strikes against both the lunar mass drivers and against the inhabited structures at the Sea of*

Tranquillity. In their testimony and in documentary evidence submitted, the surviving members of the European Space Agency ruling council at the time state repeatedly that these plans were to allow for the possibility that the lunar colonists had constructed a new accelerator of which the agency was unaware, that the agency fully understood that the authority granted to it extended only as far as making the requested preparations, and that it was not authorised at that time to execute any form of response.'

Idling over the comms logs from Earth again, Roxy sees the most recent message. Unanswered, like all the rest: *Please provide drone images of the crater patterns from the incident.*

Crater patterns? Why would Charlemagne want to see the crater patterns?

Not having anything else to do, Roxy pulls up the drone footage and tells Janus to compose an image of the surface of Epimetheus, marking where the meteor shower struck.

'It is worthy of note that several plans to strike against the lunar mass drivers were submitted. In submitting these plans, the European Space Agency made clear the balance of the risk associated with each: the risk of failure to neutralise one or more the lunar mass drivers against the risk of technical malfunction resulting in a misfire and a rogue trajectory that might result in loss of life in the settlement itself. Of these plans, the most relevant is the one that was eventually ordered: Scheme One. Scheme One required six firings, two direct strikes against each of the three mass driver sites. It is the assessment of this court, based on all evidence submitted, that the European Space Agency acted in compliance with the request made by the United Nations Security Council to propose means to neutralise a potential threat to life. The assessment of multiple contingencies, including strikes against the core Tranquillity complex, does not in itself constitute a wrong-doing.'

That much, Roxy concedes, is probably true. NEADRA had – has – trajectories prepared literally in the millions. There were lunar sites targeted sufficiently far away from any structures to be sure they wouldn't cause any damage but close enough to be seen. Contingencies for warning shots that were never used. She remembers, too, the horror she saw on the faces of the officers who'd been in the room that night as the truth of what NEADRA had done exploded into the news. She knew perfectly well what she was seeing because she'd already seen it in the mirror. She believed then and believes now that most of them had no idea of what they were about to do.

Most of them.

'The capsule from the Cronos? Is it here yet?'

'Another thirty minutes.'

'Could we redirect it to the Cronos' last position?' The capsule, at least, contains a life-support system, which is more than can be said of the Artemis drones.

'Its capability for self-propulsion is limited. Using current fuel reserves, it would take a hundred and thirty-six hours to intercept the predicted position of the Cronos based on its trajectory prior to its disappearance. It would have insufficient fuel to return.'

'Can we fuel it here?'

'Yes. But even fully fuelled, it does not have capacity to reach the last known position of the Cronos and then to return to Epimetheus.'

'But we could collect it with Artemis, and it has life support for months. Bring it in and fuel it up and get it ready to go again. As soon as you can.' Her eyes slide back to the trial. To the verdict that will damn both her and her mother.

It is again a matter of public record that the United Nations Security Council, convening in emergency session on May 21st, 2068, issued an order at 10:25pm Paris Time for the neutralisation of the lunar mass drivers, contingent on intelligence assessments that the mass drivers were uninhabited and fully automated structures, were being prepared for multiple firings, and on evidence from both NASA and the European Space Agency that these structures were sufficiently distant from the Tranquillity settlement that their destruction would not result in loss of life. This court has taken testimony from General Alexis Micah and the officers of her staff on duty at NEADRA that night. We have received and reviewed the transcript of the minutes made of a meeting between General Micah and her staff prior to General Micah issuing the fire order. In both oral and written testimonies and in the transcripts, all sources are unanimous and unambiguous: the order received by NEADRA was to execute Scheme One: target and eliminate the lunar mass drivers. This finding is consistent with further testimonies and written evidence submitted by the European Space Agency General Committee. In relation to points three and four, it is the finding of this court that the order issued to NEADRA was explicitly limited to the elimination of these mass drivers, that the preparation and issuance of this order was carried out with the correct due diligence and attention to the possibility of collateral damage and explicitly couched in terms intended to minimise loss of life. It is the finding of this court, therefore, that the fire order was a legal order. This is the order that the General Micah and her staff received and believed they had executed, up until the first impact on the Moon at 11:57pm on May 21st 2068.'

For a moment, Roxy tunes out. She doesn't hear the words from the screen. In her head, she's back in that night, to the hour that followed her mother issuing the order to take a weapon that was supposed to keep people safe from catastrophe and turn it against the Moon. Listening to the judge on her podium speaking at her lectern, anyone might be forgiven for thinking the order was given with quiet regret for its necessity, after long and careful contemplation. In Roxy's memory, the truth is very different: her mother issuing the order; several junior officers protesting. Two leaving their posts, even though they knew it would mean a court-martial. Her mother whipping them onward, pushing them to execute the order as if time were of the essence, as if they only had a slim window before the Moon started raining rocks on the defenceless Earth.

'Scheme One, for six strikes against the lunar mass drivers, was not the fire scheme executed. In this matter, the evidence presented to the court is to an extent clear: this was not a case of technical failure, of tragedy caused by flawed engineering or design. An alternative contingency trajectory referred to in the ESA minutes as Scheme Six was used, which included three additional firings targeted against Tranquillity itself. Consequently, the court has taken upon itself the duty to ask how such a failure of governance leading to such tragic consequences could occur.

Was that what happened? An error made in the frenzy, someone at a post deserted by its usual officer, perhaps, unfamiliar with their responsibility and with General Alexis Micah breathing down their neck? In hindsight, they'd had all the time in the world, but it hadn't felt that way, not that night.

It shouldn't have been possible. Everything was checked and checked again at every stage.

The judge is reaching her conclusion. Roxy tries to listen, but her thoughts keep flipping back to the night it happened, or to the empty track of void where the Cronos used to be, or to Naki lying dead in the workshop. The judge talks about a failure of governance, of ESA's "bad actor", of negligence mitigated by the fact that NEADRA, while run by the military, wasn't supposed to be a weapon, not like this. All Roxy can think of are the pictures of the aftermath. A severed limb. The image – a fake if you believe her mother – of a child dead from explosive decompression. Of Doctor Chandrasekhar, brilliant and charming and now gone. Of Naki and Karl, the three of them together raising a glass to one another after their first successful test firing. Of all the other Chandrasakhers and Nakis that might have been, the ones from the Moon, snuffed out that night by her mother's hand. They always had multiple firing solutions for multiple targets as a matter of routine: the best place to strike an incoming object, if one ever came – and they *had* come from time to time – so as deflect it or break it up. Solutions would change, sometimes from hour to hour, as new and better data arrived. They were used to that. It was what they did, constantly checking themselves...

Could it really be so banal? Surely not. Even hurling a rock at a distant planetoid, you had to be certain there was nothing in the way, no possibility of an accidental collision...

But that was why the accelerators were build where they were. Out beyond the geostationary belt. Where nothing would ever *be* in the way.

'Having reviewed the processes and procedures used, the court has determined a critical shortcoming which allows for the possibility of a firing sequence being fully checked, verified and authorised, and then being supplanted at the final stage of the process. The court has considered three possibilities. The first is human error. The second is a deliberate and malicious choice by one or more NEADRA officers, at this final stage, to select a firing sequence other than the one authorised. The third possibility, as reflected in the conclusion reached by the European Space Agency's own inquiry into the incident, is malicious action by a third party to suborn the NEADRA systems such that the sequence executed was not the sequence authorised.'

Roxy can't breathe. It's what she's always known. What her mother has always known. That weakness in the system. That very last stage. Of course, it was only obvious with hindsight, when it was too late, when hundreds of men, women and children were dead, when the agency held its own inquiry and concluded that it had been hacked.

They weren't hacked. Who would ever build a system like NEADRA and then leave it open to the possibility of such an attack? It would be like leaving nuclear launch codes on a postcard on the kitchen fridge.

'In conclusion, it is the ruling of this court that the NEADRA officers for the most part acted to execute a lawful order, and that the Tranquillity tragedy resulted either from accidental human error or from an opportunist malicious act. Either way, it is the determination of this court that a new and independent inquiry shall be convened to review the findings of the ESA internal inquiry. In addition, it is the ruling of this court that the existence of such a procedural flaw means that responsibility for the tragedy of May 21st, 2068 must lie with the European Space Agency general committee in its decision to commit the NEADRA facility to a course of action for which it was not intended, and for which its processes and controls were ineffective and inadequate.'

And so blame is allocated as expected: to the ESA general committee and thus ultimately to its President, Alessandro Serpicha, who conveniently died in a terrorist bomb three years ago, sentence carried out by the last survivors of the lunar revolutionaries. The bombers languish in prison. Will they be released? No. Of course not. No reasonable mind would even suggest it. The truth, meanwhile, will stay buried in more years of paperwork and committees and inquiries. The blame nudged with careful and contrived guidance towards a mysterious hacker. One who will never be found because they never existed in the first place.

Roxy closes her eyes. Shakes her head. That night wasn't the calm, measured, careful thing the judge describes. It was panic. It was fear. As though her mother had wanted to carry out the fire-order before anyone could change their mind.

'You rushed us into it,' she says to the void. 'You rushed us into something we shouldn't have done, and someone made a mistake, and hundreds of people died.'

'Commander,' says Janus. 'I think you need to see this.'

Replacing the images from Earth, the screen on the wall now shows the surface of Epimetheus. A bland pale grey, pock-marked with craters. The newest craters, those from the meteor shower that killed Naki, are highlighted as bright red spots. There are dozens, maybe a hundred, but the number isn't what matters. It's where they fell.

Roxy stares in disbelief. Two circular clusters of strikes. One dead centre on the Artemis Array. One centred a little off from the Earth Transmit Array, the antenna caught on the fringe. There's nothing natural about a pattern like this. Only a carefully planned act could produce such targeted precision. This was no unfortunate accident, no shower of wayward ring debris.

They have been attacked.

But how? Who? NEADRA and Epimetheus are the only accelerator arrays in existence, and NEADRA would be lucky to hit Epimetheus at all from such range. No, this had to come from somewhere much closer.

The Cronos? Is *that* why she disappeared?

That's when the alarm sounds. A quiet buzzing, warning her that somewhere in the accelerator array, one of the accelerators is firing. Roxy snaps to attention. 'Janus! Is this a drill? A test? There's nothing scheduled!' Right now, right here, is the worst possible time for such a drill, and Janus surely knows it.

'No, Commander. Someone has initiating a firing sequence.'

Day 6: 0230 hours

'Show me!' Roxy is jabbing touchscreens, as if jabbing them will make them work better, trying to call Karl as she does.

Trajectories arrange themselves on the screens around her. A one-hundred-kilogram lump of rock has just passed through the first of a planned thirty-one of the thirty-seven accelerators in orbit around Saturn. As she watches, she sees the other accelerators slowly moving. Rotating to align themselves, ready to receive their payload. The first accelerator has launched its missile towards the second. The second will catapult it towards the third. The third will hurl it onwards towards the fourth. Ever faster, each bending the trajectory until one final fling sends it on its way, rushing towards the inner system at close to a tenth of the speed of light, carrying in its kinetic energy the devastation of a twenty-megaton bomb.

Small for Saturn's accelerators, but fast.

'Where's it heading?' Janus is computing the trajectories but it's a long and difficult task, constantly being refined as the measurements of the projectile's progress provide a steadily improved estimate of its mass. By the time it reaches the last few accelerators, an estimate that's wrong by a gram either way can result in a miss by more than a thousand kilometres. The system self-corrects, monitoring the progress of its payload and making corrections up to the very last nanosecond. But it means predictions are difficult if you don't already know what you're targeting.

What it is definitely *not* doing is heading for Saturn itself, which is what it *should* be doing if this were some calibration exercise, and even that shouldn't be possible without both Roxy and Karl giving specific authorisation, which hasn't happened. And of course, there shouldn't be any *need* for Janus to predict the trajectory because Janus should know every target before any firing begins, because Janus should have set it up in the first place. But Janus hasn't, and Karl isn't answering her hails.

The rock passes through accelerator two. Its trajectory turns a little, bending towards accelerator three. The map expands to encompass the whole solar system, a line arrowing from Saturn towards the inner planets. She can see, now, where it's going. Towards Earth.

'Shut it down,' she says. 'Abort firing.'

There is a pause before Janus replies. 'I cannot, Commander. The accelerators are not responding.'

A moment as this sinks in. A moment remembering the conclusion of the ESA inquiry into the Sea of Tranquillity massacre. *We were hacked.*

'Shut all the accelerator antennas down! Cut the power!' Cutting the power won't stop the firing sequence but it means the accelerators can't make the tiny last-second corrections needed for a precision firing. She can cross her fingers and hope the mass calculations are very slightly wrong. Wrong enough, at least, for their projectile to miss its target.

A long second passes before Janus replies. 'Antennas powered down.'

'Probability of Earth intercept?' she asks.

'I estimate a fifty percent chance of impact on the Earth's surface. However, my calculations are in continual flux. I will not know the true probability until the final acceleration has completed.'

Roxy jabs her console. 'Karl! Answer the fucking comms. We have a major fucking situation here!' To Janus: 'Is there *anything* we can do to stop it?'

'No,' says Janus.

'The Cronos. It must be coming from the Cronos. It *can't* be coincidence that she disappeared.'

Why? And why bother going dark? But it *has* to be the Cronos. She appears, and then the accident that killed Naki which she now knows wasn't an accident at all, disabling their Artemis link and their ability to talk to Earth.

And now this…

Ten years ago, she was in the room when NEADRA scourged the Moon. And while it might be true that adding her own revolt to those other officers who refused her mother's orders would have made no difference, that someone else would simply have taken her place, at least her cowardice wouldn't haunt her.

'There's really no way to override the sequence once it's started?'

'There is not, Commander.'

By design, to make sure that come what may there was always a safeguard against sabotage, against remote intrusion from Earth, perhaps, or against exactly what is happening right now; except that right now she's helpless, because someone has turned their own safeguard against them.

On the trajectory screen, the projectile passes through the seventh accelerator.

'Probability of Earth intercept?' she asks again.

'Forty five percent.'

Dropping? She squeezes her eyes shut, trying to understand what that might mean. If the probability is falling, either cutting the self-correct mechanism has disturbed the trajectory enough to make it fail, or else the Cronos isn't aiming at Earth itself but at something very close.

'Contact the Cronos. Transmit at their last predicted location.'

'Commander, the accelerator antennas are still transmitting.'

'I told you to cut the power!'

'Primary power has been removed. Nevertheless, they are continuing to transmit.'

'But they can't! Not unless... Unless they have a second power source. But they don't...'

Unless someone supplied one.

The projectile has passed the twelfth accelerator. The sequence is moving fast now. Another few minutes is all she has before it completes.

The back-up batteries. The ones that are supposed to be disconnected.

Oh, shit. *Shit!*

Karl.

Karl, who's out there right now, re-establishing their link to Artemis. Who went to the surface a few days back and went to every single accelerator antenna, and even told them he'd done so.

But no, that *can't* be right! Why would Karl fire a rock at the Earth? Why would anyone except a complete madman? And she *knows* Karl. They've been out here together for long enough. She *knows* he's not mad. ESA wouldn't have sent someone who might crack under the strain of such prolonged isolation; but even if they got it wrong, she talks to him every day. She'd have seen it, and she hasn't. Whatever he's doing, he's not crazy.

Naki? The mystery of what she was doing out on the surface right before she died? But everything she thinks she knows about Karl goes double for Naki.

It's coming from outside, then. Which only leaves the Cronos.

Images of the aftermath of Tranquillity flash before her; and with them another bolt of understanding strikes. The damaged antenna array, which means they can only listen to Earth, not talk to them to warn them. The damage to the Artemis array, so there's nothing she can do to stop this. Those unscheduled calibration tests. Naki authorised them, Karl set up the trajectories. Could they have been subverted? Could they have been used as cover to throw rocks at Epimetheus? Small and slow, so it took a day for them to arrive, but targeted with pinpoint accuracy?

Not Karl. He was with her in the hub as they hit. He *knew* Naki was out there. His shock had been real enough when they discovered Naki was dead. She finds herself blinking away tears. Karl is her friend. The only friend she has out here. Possibly the only friend she has anywhere at all.

'Karl! Karl! Talk to me. You have to stop this. Please! Talk to me!'

No answer.

'The capsule from the Cronos? How far away is it?'

'Fifteen minutes from Epimetheus.'

'Show me!'

Another dot appears on the trajectory display, almost in the same orbit as Epimetheus, very close.

'Can we put it in the path of the projectile before the sequence completes? Disrupt the trajectory?' She knows the answer before Janus answers.

'No, Commander. The capsule has insufficient fuel and acceleration. Commander, we have initiated a second firing.'

'*What?*' Another projectile trajectory appears on the screen, almost identical to the first. The first accelerators are already moving, realigning themselves. 'Can we hit any of his accelerators with the capsule before his projectile reaches them? Just crash it into them if we have to?'

'No, Commander.'

'What about the accelerator antennas on Epimetheus? If we destroyed them, would that disrupt the sequence?'

'Not entirely, but it would result in a reduced probability of hitting the intended target.'

'How long before it gets here?'

'Approximately thirteen minutes.'

'And how long before the first projectile clears the last accelerator?'

'Three minutes and seven seconds.'

Nothing she can do about that one. 'And the second.'

'Between twenty-five and thirty minutes.'

'And the accelerators are definitely being controlled from Epimetheus?'

'That is correct, Commander. Sentinel is responding to commands sent from our arrays.'

So she *can* do something about the second. Roxy clenches her fists in frustration. She could suit up. Go out there. Try to shut down some of the antennas in person. Does she have time? Probably not. The capsule from the Cronos will be here before she could reach the surface.

Karl could do it, though. He's already out there.

She waits, hoping to see her monitor light up, hoping to see his face, hoping to hear him say she's wrong, that he's on it, that the Cronos is somehow behind all this. But the screen remains blank. Is he okay? She has no idea. For all she knows, the Cronos has landed outside and he's been murdered by space commandos.

'Bring the capsule from the Cronos in as fast as you can. Tell me when it's two minutes away and then give me manual control. We have access to the diagnostics from that unscheduled calibration two days ago, correct?'

'Yes, Commander.'

'What did we fire?'

'The test log records a mass of fifteen kilogrammes discharged on a trajectory directly towards Saturn. The probability that impact with Saturn did not occur is less than a trillion to one.'

'Go through the raw data. Look for anything else.' She glances at the trajectory screen. Sentinel's second projectile is on its way between the second and third accelerators.

Drones! The drones they used to look for Naki. She could punch herself for not thinking of them before. At least she can find out what's happened to Karl. 'Janus! Give me manual control of whichever of the surveillance drones is closest to Commander Veers.'

A new screen flickers to life, looking out from the little hanger on the surface of Epimetheus where the drones live. Karl hasn't gone far. He's almost right outside. She can see him, crouching beside a metal container with an antenna on top. The new Artemis array they built together only yesterday. She feels a pit of dread open inside her. A part of her had hoped to find him dead, or unconscious.

But no. There he is. Not dead. No Cronos. No space commandos.

He's the one doing this. A part of her has known this for some time, she realises. Because of the batteries in the antennas.

She launches the drone, points it, turns its tiny thrusters up as far as they can do, racing towards him, guiding it in. She's a good pilot and it's an easy target. The drone flies straight and true. The screen dies as it crashes into the Artemis antenna array.

'Give me the next drone.' One down, two to go.

A screen flickers to life and Karl's face is looking out at her.

'Hello, Roxy,' he says. 'You seem to be throwing drones at me.'

For a moment, Roxy can't speak, too busy connecting to the next drone, another still in its hanger. She can see him again now, and the antenna, too. She's damaged it, which is something.

When she finds words, they come out as a harsh whisper. 'Karl. Whatever you're doing, you need to stop.'

'And if I don't?'

'Then I'll have to do something I don't want to do.'

He nods, as if expecting this. 'I'm not sure what you have in mind. Whatever it is, I'm sorry, but you'll have to go ahead.' He gives her a little nod and a glance towards the dented antenna beside him. 'Good try, but you should have done that about ten minutes ago. I'm done with Artemis.'

'Why are you doing this?'

'Tranquillity never fired at Earth. The old SpaceX station was an abandoned folly. The Earthers blew it up to manufacture an excuse.'

'That's ridiculous.' *The Earthers…?*

'Is it?'

For all her mother's failings and those of the officers around her, Roxy can't imagine them doing something so extreme. Deliberate sabotage of an orbital station, just to give themselves an excuse?

'Yes,' she says. 'It is.'

Karl shrugs. 'And yet it happened, and they used it to deliberately target and kill my people.'

'Do you have any evidence? Because if you did, you should have made sure it reached the trial.'

Karl shakes his head. 'No evidence. Nothing concrete. But I know my people.'

My people. The second time he's used those words. 'You were on the Moon?'

'I was evacuated on the Sullenberg. We stayed in touch right to the end. They never fired at Earth. They never knew what was coming, either. NEADRA wiped them out without warning. So, I'm going to do the same. Why are you talking to me, Rox? You should be suiting up. You should be coming out here to try and stop me.'

'We both know I can't get to you in time. You're throwing rocks at Earth? You'll kill millions! If NEADRA doesn't intercept it, of course, which they very well might.'

'Not at Earth, Roxy. And not millions. Just the few who deserve it.'

'Commander,' says Janus. 'I have examined the last calibration as you requested.' A torrent of incomprehensible figures pours over the screens all around her.

'This is accelerator four during the calibration event.' A crude graphic appears of a long cylindrical object following an orbit close to Janus. Another object approaches, slowly, some random piece of space-debris Karl used for the test. As the two objects converge, the accelerator rotates, twisting on its axis so the piece of debris enters one end of the cylinder. The accelerator shifts a little in its orbit as the debris is spat out the other end, far faster than it went in. Conservation of momentum at work. The accelerator thrusters fire, stabilising the orbit. The debris hurtles off into space.

Roxy rubs her knuckles into her eyes, trying to push away the fatigue, and sees what Janus is trying to show her: another tiny puff from one of the thrusters, a full minute after its orbit has been restored.

'Rox?' Karl again. 'You still there?'

'The discharge is small enough to be an error correction,' says Janus. 'But there is also a minor power surge lasting for one tenth of a second. Individually, each of these events could be discounted as random error. However, the correlation is sufficient to suggest the discharge of a second object with a ninety percent confidence.'

So that's how he did it.

'I'm still here, Karl. I'm just looking at how you killed Naki.'

She turns back to the trajectories of Karl's projectiles. The first has passed the twenty-fifth accelerator now. Less than a minute to go. It's already travelling at a small fraction of a percent of light speed. 'What's the current probability of Earth impact?'

'Twenty-six percent. Commander, there similar anomalies from the calibration test of accelerator eight.'

Roxy turns back to Karl. 'There were never any damaged relays, were there? You set something up as an excuse to go out there and restore all the set-to-work batteries so we couldn't stop you from the hub, and to force us to run a calibration. That meteor shower that killed Naki, that was you. You hid it in the calibration.'

'I'm sorry about that. I had to shut down the Artemis array and I couldn't have us talking to Earth.'

'You killed Naki.'

'If it helps, I didn't mean to. She was supposed to be where you are now. I could have killed you, too, you know. It would have been so easy to sabotage something when you were suiting up to go outside. So, so easy. But I didn't.'

'Did you have to kill the Cronos, too? You know it was mostly filled with scientists. How did you do it? Did you put something in their path, weeks ago?'

He looks surprised. 'Nothing to do with me. She wasn't even supposed to be here. Not yet.' He shrugs. 'Maybe there was another of us on board.'

Roxy closes her eyes and sighs. She wonders how Karl managed to get himself sent here, how long he's been planning this. The Agency vets its astronauts rigorously. She, of all people, knows how stringent they are. And yet here he is, which means that everything she thinks she knows about him is a lie. The one other human being for a billion kilometres, whom she thought was her friend. 'How did you get yourself stationed here?' She knows he won't tell her.

He smiles. 'I became a new person after I came to Earth. After that, a lot of planning and a lot of waiting.'

'And a lot of help?'

He shakes his head. 'You might think that, but you know I won't answer.'

'I'm going outside when I'm done with you. In a few hours, I'll be able to talk to Earth. With luck, I'll be able to warn them before your projectiles arrive. NEADRA will shoot them down. It'll all be for nothing.'

'You don't have time.'

'Even if I don't, they'll still see it coming. They'll shoot your rock out of the stars with one of their own.'

'They'll try. Good luck, Roxy.' The screen goes dead.

'Commander,' says Janus, 'the first projectile has passed the final accelerator. The probability of Earth impact is now less than one percent. The projectile will likely pass Earth at an estimated altitude of seven hundred and twelve kilometres. A near miss, but not close enough to graze the atmosphere. Based on current manoeuvres from the accelerators, the probability of Earth impact from the second projectile is greater than ninety percent.'

Roxy stands very still. Seven hundred and twelve kilometres is the orbital altitude of the ESA command hub. The Charlemagne. The home, among other things, of...

'NEADRA. That's his target,' she says.

'There is a greater than fifty percent chance of collision with the Charlemagne Space Hub.'

'How far away is the capsule from the Cronos?'

'Six minutes, Commander.'

Does Karl expect to survive this? She supposes probably not. They don't have a brig. They don't have any contingency for this at all. Will he fire on them both before the end? Take her out with him in a blaze of glory? But if it's Earth he's after, he'll not waste precious time shifting his accelerators until he absolutely must, and she's the one buried under a hundred metres of rock and ice, while he's the one on the surface.

'Record a message. Transmit to Earth at the earliest possible opportunity, by any means that becomes available.' Roxy turns to the screen. A part of her wonders if this will be the last message she ever sends to her mother, although mostly she thinks the thought to be stupid. NEADRA isn't designed to deal with objects approaching at such speed but they'll certainly try. Even if

Karl's rocks get through, Roxy suspects her mother would probably find a way to be the last human standing.

'This is Commander Roxanne Micah broadcasting from Epimetheus Station in orbit around Saturn. Our transmit array has been damaged and out of commission for the last three days.' She checks the time. 'At oh-two twenty-seven hours UTC, Epimetheus executed a firing sequence. The target appears to be the ESA Charlemagne station.' Her breath catches as she says the name. Last she knew, her mother is there. 'I have continued to receive transmissions from Earth and have no reason to believe this firing to be sanctioned. The projectile is in-bound at approximately ten percent of light speed. The estimated mass of the projectile is one hundred kilogrammes. The estimated energy of impact is approximately twenty megatons. The estimated flight time is nine hours and fifty minutes.'

She stops and stares into the empty screen. It's always strange, talking this way, knowing she could be dead before her words are ever heard. That, more than anything else, is what makes Epimetheus so isolating. Doctor Chandrasekhar's QIF technology will change that. It will change space travel forever.

Doctor Chandrasekhar will never see it happen.

She's shaking. Anger.

'Janus, suspend recording. ETA on the capsule?'

'Four minutes.'

'Resume. Epimetheus command has been unable to disrupt the firing sequence. Epimetheus is attempting to effect action to restore control over the Sentinel accelerators. We continue to monitor all channels for instructions. Please respond to acknowledge you have received this transmission.' She pauses again. 'In addition, the Cronos disappeared from all sensors approximately sixty minutes ago and is not responding to attempts at communication. We fear her lost with all hands.'

We. Why does she refer to herself as 'we' in all this? But she knows the answer. Denial. Denial that she's so very, very alone.

She ends the transmission and turns to Janus. 'ETA on the capsule?'

'Three minutes, Commander.'

She leans back, forcing herself to remember her own time on the Charlemagne, working under her mother's command. A part of her, she discovers, is glad the station will die. That was where she was when her mother murdered the Moon. They'll have time to evacuate. Three hours was the best they'd managed in simulation and drills. Three hours to clear everyone onto the escape shuttles. Their own telescopes should give them plenty of warning so no one will have to die. She wonders, briefly, if that was what Karl wanted all along. The destruction of Charlemagne, a statement of revenge, but no one dead.

Except… people *will* die. Charlemagne's escape pods are little more than re-entry capsules or orbital lifeboats, designed to save the crew in case of some catastrophic internal failure that cripples the station. The impact of a hundred kilogrammes of rock travelling at ten percent of the speed of light will shatter the station into a million fragments, each with an energy and a momentum of its own, a cone of destruction spreading through Earth orbit along the vector of the impact. Anything nearby will get caught in a hail of debris. It won't stop there, either. Thousands of fragments, sent into a chaos of elliptical orbits, wreaking havoc for years before they can all be caught and tamed.

And that's just the beginning.

On the trajectory display, Karl's second projectile reaches the fourth accelerator. Its mass has increased now, amplified by velocity and relativity. The first is already racing away on the final leg of its journey to Earth.

'Janus. Restore primary power to the accelerator antennas and give me manual capsule control,' she says. 'Karl? Are you still there?'

A moment passes, and then Karl's face flashes onto her screen again. Roxy blinks in shock and then dismay. He has a look to him that she's never seen. A hardness.

'Hello Karl,' she says.

'It's done,' he says. 'Come and get me.'

'If I do, does it stop?'

He shrugs. 'Shut me down and you get back control, so yes, I suppose it does, if you can do that. But... Rox, you're still in the hub.'

'Abort the second firing, Karl. I know the first isn't targeting Earth but the second is. You're already going to destroy the Charlemagne. Let that be enough.'

'That's where they are. The people who killed the Moon. That's where they've been while this trial was going on. Hiding in orbit where no one could reach them in case the verdict wasn't what they wanted.'

'They'll evacuate,' she says. 'They'll see it coming and they'll abandon the station.'

'I know.' He seems unfazed, as if she's somehow missing the point.

'So, you destroy their station. That's your revenge?'

'A part of it, at least.'

'They'll only build another. And NEADRA protects the Earth from everything.'

'Not from me, it doesn't.'

'They could throw a rock back at us, you know.'

'I suppose they could, but it really doesn't make any difference now.'

On the console in front of her, she can see the surface of Epimetheus through the eyes of the capsule from the Cronos. Two minutes away. The trajectory loaded by Janus wants to use the thrusters to slow down, to bring the capsule in nice and easy. Roxy overrides the instructions and starts a hard burn.

'Karl... You know I used to work for NEADRA.'

'You almost had to have worked there to be sent here,' he says. 'I worked there too. For a while.' He smiles. She doesn't know why. 'I even met your mother.' The smile stays on his lips as his eyes glitter with ice.

'I was there when NEADRA fired on the Moon. I was in the control room.' She watches his face now, looking for a reaction but sees nothing. 'I was the one. It was me. I loaded the trajectories and committed the accelerators to fire. I did it. I was the last link in the chain. It was my mistake. I killed them. Me.'

She remembers it as though it were yesterday. Always has. All of it, except the critical moment. The pre-firing checks are completed. The final simulations too. Her monitor is blinking at her: *Confirm Firing.* Her own final checks that the correct sequence had been selected. Everything is as it should be. She's sure of it.

Her mother standing over her. *You can let me, if you prefer...*

But no, she was an officer with a duty and responsibility. *No. I'll do my duty, ma'am.*

And then... Nothing.

Another burn from the capsule, lifting it up higher over the surface. She's over the horizon now. If Karl looks up, he might even see her, a bright speck in the night sky, moving too quickly to be a star or even a stray piece of debris from Saturn's rings.

'It wasn't a conspiracy, Karl. It was a mistake. An accident. I checked it three times and I don't know how I got it wrong, but I did. That's why I'm here. Because of the trial, because it keeps me away where no one can reach me, or touch me, or talk to me. And because they know I'll do it right, if I ever have to do something like that again. I'm sorry, Karl. I've lived with the guilt of that night for a decade. But it wasn't a conspiracy. It was a mistake. That's all.'

She can never quite remember the moment she pressed the screen. Did a finger slip, in that instant when she looked away? Was that how it happened?

For long time, Karl stays silent. 'It was really you?' he says at last.

'Yes.'

'Am I supposed to forgive you?'

'It wouldn't matter even if you did.'

He smirks a little, the first hint of cruelty she's ever seen in his face. 'No, Roxy. Nice try, but I don't buy it.'

Another burst, and then the start of a last long burn. She can see the station below her now, rushing closer.

'I don't care.' She's shocked by the unexpected truth of her own words. 'It's just something that needed to be said to another human being. Someone who understands the weight of it.'

Karl shakes his head. 'They'll evacuate the station. And yes, I know that most of them will get out in orbital lifeboats and wait for someone to pick them up, but not *all* of them. The officers and generals and the senior staff, the ones responsible, *they* won't want to sit adrift in orbit for a week. They'll take one of the shuttles. Where to the shuttles go, Roxy? You were stationed there, so you know the evacuation protocols.'

'Kourou.'

'Kourou in French Guiana. Home to more than a hundred years of ESA history. Do you know how long it takes for a shuttle from Charlemagne to make the transit and land?'

'About six hours.'

'The second rock will hit as they land. They won't see it coming. They'll all die. Every single one of those war criminals will die. It's what they deserve, Roxy. For what they did.'

'Naki never saw it coming either.'

'I'm sorry about Naki. Sometimes people get hurt who don't deserve it. Sometimes it's the only way to get anyone to listen.'

And sometimes no one hears at all. 'And all the people who work and live in Kourou? It's a city. People live there who had nothing to do with this. Do *they* deserve it?'

'I'm sorry about that. They –'

'Goodbye, Karl.'

She cuts the comms. She can still see him, in the video feed from the capsule. A siren is sounding. Janus is shouting impact warnings. The doors to the armoured survival suits have opened; but Roxy barely notices any of this. She only has eyes for Karl, as he looks up at the last moment, impact only a second away, and sees what's coming.

She closes the screen.

The hub shakes, hard and violent. Several monitors go dead. Janus shouts warnings and alarms. She catches something in there about life support, about an integrity breach. For a few long seconds she simply sits and does nothing. It's the easy way out. Let it all happen. Let Karl have his revenge. Let the air drain out of Epimetheus, and her with it. The last moments of Roxanne Micah.

Tempting…

'Janus. Abort the firing.'

She kicks herself out of the seat and towards the nearest of the armoured emergency suits. She can feel the air getting thinner as it seals itself around her, a safe cocoon.

She'll have to talk to her mother again. Say her goodbyes. After that, find a way to talk to Earth that isn't the encrypted link to the Charlemagne. She has a confession to make, after all, and everyone needs to hear. She has no idea how to say any of that, but for now it doesn't matter. If the station isn't damaged beyond repair, she might even survive. Janus will keep her in air and water. She has food for years. In six months, the *Voyager* will arrive.

If she's still here when it comes.

Did she really make a mistake? She's never quite shaken the idea that her mother changed the sequence as she stood at her daughter's shoulder, in the moment Roxy looked up at her, or is that simply the desperation of the guilty, looking for a way out?

She'll never know. And really, does it even matter now?

As she thinks on this, she starts to sing to herself, quiet and out of tune.

'*Wipe away the tears, wash away the blood, regrets are like a river, grief is like a flood…*'

About the Author

Stephen Deas was born in Southeast England, in 1968, and mostly brought up in a town full of retired colonels. His early memories largely consist of running around building sites and being able to spell 'colonel' at an unusually early age. Like most people of that age, he took to making up imaginary friends to supplement his real ones. *Un*like most people, he never stopped. Deas is the author of more than twenty novels covering fantasy (which he writes under his own name and as Nathan Hawke), crime (as SK Sharp), science fiction (as Sam Peters, or as Gavin Deas when co-authoring with Gavin Smith) and historical fiction (as SJ Deas). As well as his novel works, Deas is desperately trying to convince Netflix that what it really needs is a show centred on Irene Adler.

Aside from writing books, Deas has, at various times, been obsessed with mathematics, classical piano music, kung-fu, particle physics and Sid Meier's Civilisation (the original). Anything that explodes is fascinating, rockets are irresistible, but those are genetic things and thus Not His Fault. He now lives in Essex with his wife and two boys where he continues to pretend to be other people, most frequently A Responsible Parent(TM).

NP Novellas

2: Worldshifter – Paul Di Filippo
High-octane SF reminiscent of Jack Vance but wholly Di Filippo in its execution. Klom is forced into a desperate chase across the stars, pursued by the most powerful beings in the galaxy, after he stumbles on a secret in the bowels of an antique ship.

3: May Day – Emma Coleman
Orphaned during wartime at just seventeen, May continues with the silly superstitions her mum taught her. Until the one time she doesn't; at which point something dark and deadly arises, and proceeds to invade her life, determined to claim her as its own...

4: Requiem for an Astronaut – Daniel Bennett
30 years ago, astronaut Joan Kaminsky disappeared while testing an experimental craft powered by alien technology. Now, her glowing figure starts to appear in the sky, becoming a focus for anti-tech cults. One man, who knew Joan, determines to find out why.

5: Rose Knot – Kari Sperring
Kari Sperring, historian and award-winning fantasy author, delivers a gripping tale of love, infidelity, loyalty, misguided intentions and the price of nobility, featuring some lesser known members of Arthur's court: the sons of Lot, the Orkney royal family.

6. On Arcturus VII – Eric Brown
Former pilot and planetary pioneer Jonathan James is lured back to the one place he vowed never to return to: Arcturus Seven. A Closed Planet; a world where every plant and animal is hell-bent on killing you; the place that cost him the life of the woman he loved.